LETTERS FROM THE LAND OF LA

a collection

JOSIE LYNN

FootePrint Press
California, USA

Published by FootePrint Press.

Publisher's Cataloging-In-Publication Data

Names: Lynn, Josie

Title: Letters from the land of la / Josie Lynn

Description: [Manteca], California, USA : FootePrint Press, [2016] | Letters from the land of la | Fiction. | Contents: Fan mail — La-la land — Blue lights — Summer flies — The wedding dress — Too many people — Elevator music — Peanut butter soup — Black out — Thin ice — Intended purpose.

Identifiers: LCCN 2016932490 | ISBN 978-0-9904353-0-3

FAN MAIL

High energy is how Ginger always described her father, in and out of her life from the day she could remember. Saturdays would start off leisurely with a quiet breakfast with her mother. Then he would whisk in, just down from his shower or just in from an all-night rehearsal, saying, "Let's take the boat out today," or "What a great day for a picnic!" and she and her mother would rush to catch up.

She and her mother would spend Sunday mornings reading the newspaper, debating over whether they wanted pancakes or waffles and he would rush in, kissing them both before rushing off somewhere—a rehearsal this week, the airport next week—anywhere but his seat at the head of the table, lit from behind by the morning sun, shinning like the god she believed him to be, leaving in his wake the static of his presence and the lingering scent of his cologne.

Sometimes, when Ginger tried to remember those days before the divorce, all she could see was her father's figure, retreating into the shadows.

After the divorce, she only saw him on rare occasions, and when she did, he still seemed to be in perpetual motion.

The car would be running outside and Ginger would shove her weekend clothes into a duffel bag, zipping it closed as she ran. "Tick tock, tick tock," he would say. "I'm growing old." It wasn't true; he was eternally young. Boyish, the articles always said. Boyish grin, boyish charm, boyish good-looks. "Let's go, already," he would say, rushing their weekends, rushing their summers, until it was all a tangled-up mass of unsorted memories.

Time sped along, turning days into weeks, weeks into months, months into years, all set to her father's frantic beat. She was forever running to keep up, desperately trying to catch up, to savor and remember it all, never certain what she missed, only over-hearing it in whispered snippets and inside jokes.

His music was the one constant in her life, the one thing that made it seem as if he'd never left. She would put his records on, and he would explode from the speakers with frenetic guitar riffs and enigmatic lyrics that she never could decipher, but seemed to hint at a perfect world where everyone was happy, beautiful, young, and in love. His videos—always full of beautiful, young models who were always kissing him—exuded life and energy, and bold, brash brilliance.

Ginger could never forgive Sara for allowing her father to leave, taking all the sunshine with him, and casting her in the role of visitor. Visitor Number One, perhaps, but visitor just the same.

She could never forgive him for showing more regard for

her half-brother Sherman than he did for her. She could not forgive the fact that she and Sherman were born in the same year, only months apart, even though Billy hadn't left her mother until Ginger was four. For four years he'd led two lives, had two families, and hers had been the lie. For four years he had not had the character to choose, but when he finally did, he'd chosen someone else.

Sometimes Billy would give Ginger's name as his publicist. Calls would come in from magazines and newspapers seeking interviews, and Ginger would know he was coming to town.

When Ginger entered the house, she went straight to the corner, ignoring Billy's two stepdaughters and Sherman. Ginger had never gotten along with kids her age. Billy vaguely remembered that it had, on occasion, caused him some concern. Then he remembered he usually let Sara worry about such matters.

It struck him as odd how little Ginger and Sherman resembled each other. They were so close in age they might as well be twins, but they were night and day.

Sherman looked like him, but had his mother's build. Ginger was thin and wispy, like Billy, but had her mother's exquisite features. She was a real beauty; Sherman was ordinary.

She was wonderful, Billy often thought. She always had been. He remembered her as a child—sweet and caring.

She'd look at him and her face would light up, and he would know that he was her world, she adored him, and it had been all he needed. He was the sun, the life-giver—the source of energy and warmth.

After he left, her eyes always seemed to be searching him, accusing him in their sweet way. Sometimes he thought she could sense what he feared most, and he knew his smile, though brilliant, would not be enough to cover it. She was reading him as her mother always could.

Sometimes he wondered why she hadn't done something more spectacular with her life. She was, after all, his daughter. Then he would realize that—sitting alone in the corner, removed from the limelight that he so craved—the solitude agreed with her, and it would occur to him that she was as foreign to him as her mother had always been.

At odd moments, he would catch the gaze from her deep and wistful eyes and it would be as if a shadow had passed between them. Then he would know that her faith in him was wavering. He would look away, and it would be several moments before he would have the courage to meet her gaze again. When he did, he would see that she was smiling and he would know that he had not ruined her life. She was Billy Edwards' daughter. How many kids could claim that?

He was walking towards Ginger now, smooth and light, charming and debonair. "How's college? Is there an end in sight?" He was flirting. He couldn't help himself.

"I've decided to go back for another year," she said.

"I see." He was annoyed, she could tell. "And whatever

happened to teaching?"

"I was only substituting. And I didn't like it. I'm doing volunteer work now."

"Volunteering, huh? That's means no pay, right? How about volunteering around here? Kate could use some help opening my fan mail."

He was turning on the charm, as if she was just another female fan, and she was buying into it, she could tell, although she tried to resist, because as much as she wanted to deny it, when he smiled, all living things turned to him.

He was running away again. She had always suspected it, and then one day, he told her.

"Kate and I have to get away. We have to have our own life. The whole time we've been married, there've always been these other people, her kids, my kid, our kid, the band, my managers. We need to be alone together."

They were moving to New York. The studio was talking about releasing a greatest hits album. This could be the year. This could be his comeback.

So go, Ginger thought. *I don't need you.*

She stood among the crowd at his farewell concert. She preferred to watch him with the crowd, instead of backstage with the rest of the friends and family. She'd rather watch him amid strangers.

She would watch him, mesmerized, just like everyone else in the room, feeling a part of the collective consciousness.

He was in control of the crowd, of their thoughts and their emotions. No matter what he did, they would always come back for more.

They had been promised a show, and Billy Edwards could not disappoint. No matter how empty he had ever left her feeling, when she watched him on the stage, Ginger could not believe he had ever been capable of disappointing.

The room was dark and noisy, electric with excitement, filled with the smell of smoke, sweat, and alcohol. The lights lowered and when they came up, her father was on the stage. Suddenly, in an explosion of sound, the show began.

Ginger listened, her heart racing, driven by the permeating beat of the room. The music never would end, not like the structured classical pieces she'd been taught as a child. This music just kept grinding along in a mad, furious, circular path, going nowhere, taking them nowhere.

The performance was history the moment it came to life. You could never stand on equal terms to face it. Chasing it was futile. You could try to hold it between your fingers, but it would slip through, just as if it had never happened. You thought, perhaps, you had imagined it all.

The music antagonized her. She had never liked it. A song or two, here and there, perhaps, but she had never been a diehard fan, not like the people around her. She'd just happened to grow up in his world.

There were times she wondered if she existed apart from Billy Edwards and his waves of adoring fans, or if she was just another nameless face in his crowd. She was glad he was going back to New York.

Once he left, she surreptitiously reentered her regular life, hoping her mother wouldn't notice her absence. She would pick up right where she left off, the Saturday morning breakfasts, the Sunday night Bunco games with her mother's friends.

"What's Miss Ginger up to these days?" they would ask. "Any new boyfriends?" Before she could answer, they'd be off, bragging about their daughters, who were all Ginger's age and, by their mothers' accounts, were all leading glamorous, exciting lives.

She would return to school to the friends who all would stare at her with the same fascinated look when they found out she was Billy Edwards' daughter. "What was it like growing up with him?" they would ask.

"I'll let you know when he grows up," she would answer.

By the time her father called to invite her to spend a few weeks at his new home, she did not have the strength to turn him down. San Francisco was dark, Sara was dull, and Ginger was suffering from ennui.

Kate would be waiting for her at the airport. "Kiss, kiss," she would say, air-kissing her on either side. She'd smile. It would be friendly enough, but it would remind Ginger of the first time they'd met.

Kate had been charming and sparkling, as always, not at all like Sara. "This is my new wife," Billy had said, grinning broadly. He might as well have said, "This is my new life."

Ginger saw Kate's two children staring at her from behind

their mother, and then they all began to retreat.

Please, Daddy, please don't go! she'd wanted to yell.

She woke up with a jolt as the plane landed. The seat belt light was off, and passengers were starting to mill around the cabin. Ginger stared blindly at the tarmac. Kate would be waiting for her at baggage claim.

Kate was throwing one of her parties that night, and she made no attempt to conceal the fact that she viewed Ginger's arrival as a tremendous inconvenience. She'd had to change into her 'picking someone up at the airport outfit.' That meant she'd have to change back into her 'pre-party outfit' once she got home, only to change into her 'party outfit' later that evening. She waved her hands and arms as she spoke. She took up a lot of negative space.

When Ginger offered to help with the preparations, Kate made it clear that there was going to be nothing she could do that would please her, and that she was more of a hindrance than help. So, after a few angry words with Kate and Billy, Ginger left the apartment.

Taryn DeJong, her friend from high school, was in New York, working as a photographer for a fashion magazine.

They'd been texting each other for the last few years, so when Ginger decided to leave the house, contacting Taryn was her first thought.

"Guess what," she texted. "I'm in the Big Apple, and the Big Chill is on."

"Corner bar. Drinks on me," was the instant reply.

The next thing Ginger knew, she was sitting in a bar

listening to Taryn's laughter as she described her fight with Kate.

"Oh, poor Baby," Taryn said. "If I could have your problems—a father living in only one of the poshest neighborhoods in Soho, free room and board. I bet you even have your own terrace."

"I do," Ginger said, laughing.

"I thought so. Only a wicked stepmother to mar your otherwise untainted bliss."

"Did I ever tell you what a comfort it is to have sympathetic friends?"

"I'm telling you, Ginger, I could totally deal with that. By the way, you'll never guess who's here. It's practically a class reunion."

For the first time Ginger noticed the man sitting to Taryn's left. He was leaning over Taryn toward her, looking at her. Ginger had seen that face countless times.

When she traveled abroad at night, most nights, she'd look out of the dark train windows and stare into her sad, lonely eyes. But some nights, when her tired mind was playing tricks on her, those eyes seemed to morph, and he would be staring back at her, searching for something.

"Ginger Edwards, do you remember me?"

Ginger felt her face flush. "Dale Spencer! I don't believe it's really you."

He was dressed like a banker but grinned like a school boy. He stood up and walked over towards her.

"Do I, at least, get a hug? I came all this way just to see

you. That's at least worth a hug."

"I just can't believe it's Dale Spencer."

"You keep saying that. Tell me, is this a good or bad reaction? I mean, I've been known to have both effects on people."

"No, I just honestly never thought I'd see you again."

"Yet, here I am in living color. What have you been doing with yourself? Don't answer that, I can see." Dale stepped back to look at Ginger. "You look...great."

"Taryn, you didn't tell me. So, how long have you and Dale been together?"

"We're not—You thought he and I were—? No." Taryn was emphatic.

"Worse things could happen to you, you know," Dale said.

"Believe me, they have." Taryn said, laughing.

"I'm sorry guys, I guess I just assumed."

"Oh, a natural assumption, Ginger." Taryn said. "Dale and I are just two misplaced Californians who found each other in this cesspool of a city and decided to get smashed."

"Well, I hope you, at least, had the decency to wait for me."

"Allow me." Dale handed Ginger a beer and sat down next to her. "Drink up," he told her. "You've got some catching up to do. Speaking of catching up, you're the only reason I ever feel the need to drink. Remember how you treated me in high school? You ignored me mercilessly, and I never got over it."

"I have no recollection of that."

Taryn laughed. "Something tells me that's my cue. I'll text you, Ginger. Maybe we can grab a bite, or something, tomorrow. I have to get back to work, anyway. I'm due at a fashion shoot." Taryn rolled her eyes and left.

Once they were alone, Dale turned to Ginger, still smiling, as if he would never stop. "Ginger, you grew up good. You always were my ideal, you know. And you've just gotten better."

"You must be really drunk, Dale. How many of these have you had?"

"I'm sorry, but you have this effect on me. When I get within five feet of your vicinity my edit button malfunctions, and I start spewing out unfiltered honesty. I always told myself I'd act cool and dignified if I ever saw you again, but I feel just like a 16-year-old kid, which, incidentally is how old we were the last time we saw each other."

"That's what I remember about you, your imagination. So, not to change the subject, but—"

"No, please do."

"What brings you to New York?"

"Well, my firm is opening an East Coast branch, and they sent me to help organize one of the departments."

"I see you're still the indispensable Dale Spencer. Nothing ever changes, does it?"

"I'd like to think some things can. You can't imagine how many times I've thought of you over the years."

"I've thought of you a lot, too, Dale."

"I mean, I had the biggest crush on you in high school. All the boys did."

"That's not quite the truth, Dale. You're slightly delusional. I was pretty much nondescript back then. Like I said, not much has changed."

"No, all the boys definitely had crushes on the aloof, elusive Ginger Edwards. Why do you think I remember you all these years later?"

"Because we were friends, Dale."

"No, we were classmates. We were never friends. You didn't let people get close to you."

"The teen years were hard. But, let's not talk about that. Let's talk about you."

Growing up, there had been several false starts. Several times, she'd lost who she was, most notably in seventh grade, the year she met Mario.

Third period science. Mr. Bellfry asked the class what was the speed of light. Mario blurted out an answer which, of course, was wrong. Ginger turned to give him a look that said, 'you idiot.' Then she caught a glimpse of him. He was beautiful. He sensed her stare, gave her a cocky smile, then winked and shrugged. Ginger turned away. She never spoke to him again, but she watched, dreamed, hoped, and planned.

Eighth grade had been particularly painful because she and her mother had to give up their house and move to an apartment. She had to change schools, and that meant leaving Mario. His life went on without her. He started dating some girl. Actually, her name was Jill McGraw. Ginger thought she would remember that name until the day she died.

That was the year she didn't make the honor roll, the year her mother seemed to spend the entire year watching her out of frightened eyes. Ginger fell into a slump of depression that lasted two years. Sara noticed, and was frantic with worry.

Ninth grade meant new friends, Taryn and Dale. Tenth grade was the year she started high school, and was reunited with Mario, at least, they were in the same school again. The fact that he didn't notice her any more in high school than he had in seventh grade did not squelch her obsessive interest in him. Her eyes followed his every move, her every moment was consumed with thoughts of him—handsome Mario, popular Mario, self-centered and conceited Mario.

Now it seemed to her that she'd spent an inordinate amount of time thinking about, wondering about, worrying about some boy she didn't even speak to now. It had been a grand waste of time, but what else had there been to do?

In eleventh grade, she met a modeling agent at the mall and he successfully talked Sara into letting her model. That was the first time she listened when someone called her beautiful, the first year she could look in the mirror and actually believe it of herself.

Looking back, there were moments so painful they were burned into her secret thoughts. These were the thoughts that kept her going in her loneliest hours. She'd recall all the disappointments, all the great hopes, and all the big dreams.

Sometimes it seemed they'd all come crashing down at once with a reverberating thud, but they kept her moving forward, as stubborn and as insistent as the motion of a train, which she could feel long after she had disembarked.

Sitting in the bar with Dale, she recalled their last meeting. Tenth grade. It had been raining. Her mother was waiting for her in the office with bad news: they were moving, again.

As usual, Dale was waiting for her so they could walk to trig together. She had to tell Dale she wasn't going to class, but at that moment, she saw Mario walking toward her.

Dale was smiling. "Can I have a hug?" he asked. He'd never hugged her before, but it was fortuitous because Mario happened to be watching.

So she hugged Dale, while she watched Mario. She hugged him, never suspecting it would be the last time she would see him, never suspecting it would be the last image Mario would have of her, never suspecting how empty she would feel for trying to use Dale to make Mario jealous.

She would be on the night train from Paris, staring out the blackened window. The rest of the car would be asleep, and as she stared into her eyes, it would be as if she could see into her core. On those lonely train rides, the only one she ever thought about was Dale.

"What's going on in that brain of yours?" Dale asked.

Ginger looked up. There were tears in her eyes.

Dale clasped her hand and squeezed it.

"I was remembering the last time I saw you," she said simply.

"I remember. It was raining. And your hair was curling up around your face."

Billy was giving a concert on Dale's last night in New York. Dale wanted to take Ginger to the theater, but she asked him to come with her to the concert instead.

"He's pretty good," he yelled across the table. He was smiling, caught up in the intoxicating beat.

"Don't tell me you're a disciple too," she said.

"Hey, this was your idea, remember? I wanted to see *Les Miz*."

Once Ginger returned home, she began teaching again. She and Dale would talk on the phone well into the night. At work, they would text each other, making plans for the weekend, but something would inevitably come up.

Finally, Ginger sent a text to Taryn. "What's up with Dale? Is he married?"

"You tell me what's up with him. You're the one he has the 'thing' for," was Taryn's less than helpful reply.

Dale left a message on her cell phone the next day.

"You wanted to speak to me," she said when he answered. "You sounded serious."

"I don't know how to say this, other than to just say it. You know how I feel about you. That makes this difficult."

"You're breaking up with me?" she whispered.

"I don't want to. But anything else wouldn't be fair." His voice broke. "Why is it when I want to seem cool and dignified in front of you, I just can't?"

"What is it, Dale?"

"Ginger, I've been waiting for you my whole life."

"Me, too."

"So, I guess just saying it would be the thing. But how...?"

"Dale," Ginger said, "you're scaring me."

"The thing is...before we met...when I was a kid, I used to get sick a lot."

"Okay," Ginger said because he paused and it seemed appropriate.

"And then it turned out that I was really sick. I had cancer."

"Oh, no!"

"But I was one of those success stories. I fought it. And I won. I put it behind me. I'd had cancer. Past tense. I was a survivor.

"I was convinced that I was lucky. Then I ran into to you, the girl of my dreams, and I guess I thought I was one of those guys whose luck doesn't run out.

"The only trouble is, it does."

"Dale! What are you saying?"

"I hadn't been feeling myself for a while now, and I was afraid to find out what was wrong. When I saw you again, everything changed. I started caring about things I hadn't cared about in a long time. So I decided to go in for some tests, just to make sure everything was all right. But it isn't. Ginger, it's back. I don't have much time."

"I don't know what you mean," she finally said, because

she couldn't think of anything else to say.

"I have cancer. The doctors are going to treat it. I want to fight it, Ginger. I have too much to live for now. But, realistically—"

"How long do you have?" It amazed Ginger how calm her voice sounded, calm and matter-of-fact, as if they were discussing the weather.

"Six months. Maybe."

"Then we'll have to get married right away," she said.

"I wanted to spend the rest of my life with you. But seeing how short a time that is, it seems cruel and unfair to ask that of you."

"But you didn't, Dale. I did."

They had a small, private wedding. Sara was Ginger's only guest. It felt awkward to include both her mother and Billy. Since she had to choose, she chose Sara. Dale invited his boss.

Sara cried. She kept saying that a wedding was the beginning of something, not the end, but Ginger knew that it could be both.

They honeymooned in Tahiti because Ginger remembered a poster she had seen in a travel agency when she was seven. Billy and Kate were living in Hawaii that year, and Ginger was supposed to spend the summer with them. The thought of spending a whole summer with Billy and Kate made Ginger feel alone. She remembered sitting on the cold, metal folding chair at the travel agency, looking longingly at the poster of Tahiti hanging above the desk, thinking she would prefer to go to Tahiti with someone who loved her.

As they walked along the beach, Dale told Ginger about his parents' beach house.

"It's where we used to spend our summers. I haven't been there since Mom died, but I'd like to see it again."

When they returned to San Francisco, they took the short drive up the coast to the beach house. It was dusty and slightly weathered, but otherwise just as Dale remembered. Ginger went outside to find wood for the fire, and when she returned, she found Dale sitting on the floor in the corner.

She sat beside him and took his hand. "Who says we have to go back? You've got savings and insurance. Let's cash it in. We can stay here."

Dale nodded. "I was thinking, this is where I want to spend the rest of my life."

Dale was lying on the sofa, listening as Ginger played the piano.

"I always loved you," he said, "long before you noticed me."

"You paid too much attention to me. I didn't trust that." She stopped playing and sat on the floor beside the sofa.

"Why do you even like me?" she asked quietly.

"What a question. How could anyone who knows you help but like you?" He took her hand. "The thing I remember most about you was when you stood up for Natasha, the girl all of the popular girls bullied. You were this quiet, little person, but you sure had a big mouth when it counted."

"I don't remember that," Ginger said.

"You stood up for her the way you never stood up for yourself. I never forgot it and I'm sure Natasha never did, either."

"What will I do without you?" Ginger asked.

Dale kissed her. "Thrive," he said.

One morning Ginger awoke to find Dale sitting in a chair on the deck. He hadn't slept well, and the rain had awoken him.

"Let's go for a walk," he said softly.

Ginger got her jacket and helped him walk down the stairs to the beach. He seemed smaller, as if he were disappearing.

"Do you regret these six months? Investing all this time in something that wasn't going to last?"

"I would do it a million times over, even if I knew it would end this way every time."

"I can't stop thinking that you deserve better than this, Ginger."

"No, Dale, I'm trying hard to convince myself that I deserve you."

Neither of them said anything. Ginger watched a group of sandpipers making tracks in the sand.

"I want you to know that I'll never re-marry," she said.

"But I want you to, Ginger. I want you to be happy, and to have children. You'll be a phenomenal mom. Promise me you won't give up on love."

"No one will ever love me like you do. And it's enough,

Dale." They'd promised not to cry, but she could not fight it anymore.

Dale hugged her. "I love the way your hair curls up when it rains," he said, and when she didn't answer, he added, "Don't you hate sad, long, drawn-out good-byes?"

When it was time to bury him, Ginger made sure there was no fanfare, only a simple funeral that was as real and as sincere as Dale had been. Afterwards, she went home to pack up the beach house. She'd get an apartment in the city, find a job, and try to resume a life.

One of Sara's friends who hadn't seen Ginger in a while asked, "What have you been up to, Ginger?" Sara glanced anxiously at Ginger.

"Teaching," Ginger said. "Living."

"Sounds boring," the friend said, laughing.

"It is," Ginger said.

When Billy came to town again, Ginger tried to ignore his coming but, as usual, found herself sucked in by the whirlwind his presence always created.

She watched the concert from the audience. She was looking on with the rest of the fans, when Billy called Sherman and his girlfriend to the stage.

"I want you all to meet someone I'm very proud of," Billy said. "My son's about to make me a grandfather."

The audience cheered and shouted congratulations, as Ginger looked on.

A life, a death, a birth, it was all part of the heartless circle. She wished she and Dale had been able to raise a child together. Somehow Sherman always managed to get the things she wanted.

Everyone was going back to the house with Billy and Kate, and Ginger followed.

She sat at the bar, staring at her drink, as Billy approached and sat down. She could tell it was him without looking up by the way he smelled and the way he stood too close to her.

She remembered how she used to wonder, when she was small, why he never asked her to sing with the band. She was always at the concerts, and he knew she could sing.

"I sing," she said.

"Do you?" he asked. He sounded distracted.

"Yes," she said. "I'm really quite good." She started to cry. "I shouldn't have come. I'm sort of not in the mood for this anymore."

"I know. I'm sorry, Ginger. I really am." She wondered why he didn't hug her. But someone came over to congratulate him on the show, and he was busy lighting up their world.

Ginger started to stand, but Billy grabbed her hand.

"Please," she said. "Let me go."

The sun was setting when she got to the beach. She sat in her car and watched the waves etch intricate patterns in the sand. She pondered the pointlessness of the exercise, since their work lasted only as long as it took for new waves to move in to wash away their traces.

Gradually darkness descended upon the beach. The stars

were rising, twinkling in their brilliance. The planets were brighter, but only the stars sparkled with their own light.

Finally, because she waited long enough, she saw a shooting star. She imagined it burning a path across the sky, dripping a trail of sparks into the ocean.

Ginger cried quietly. Brief though it was, it had been worth it.

LA-LA LAND

"Hollywood's not a place, it's an idea," Mom used to say. Looking back, I don't know what she would know about that. She'd never held on to either a place or an idea long enough to do her or anyone else any good.

She was wrong, though. Hollywood was very much a place—vividly real, shockingly alive, and as disappointing as any place on earth. I know, because I lived there.

We'd come from Tennessee, once upon a time, once Mom had exhausted that state's seemingly endless supply of deadbeat boyfriends—real losers—the kind of man you wouldn't trust with your dog, but Mom let these creeps into our lives without a second thought. We finally settled somewhere in California's Central Valley at the home of a kindly relation who offered sanctuary while Mom's latest ex forgot he was looking for us.

My first trip to Hollywood had been as a tourist. Dad was in town on business sometime before he disappeared once and for all in Mexico, long before I thought love was just another four-letter word. He blew in, in his light blue

Skylark—a perfectly named vehicle for Dad, who was always off on some lark or another. He whisked me off to Hollywood, casually pointing out a few points of interest that we'd sail past between business calls. He'd point out Mann's Chinese Theater, the Hollywood sign, stop at a business, show his catalogs, then he'd be off again, modern-day traveling medicine show that he was.

Afterwards we'd have lunch. We'd talk, Dad and I, about anything and everything and nothing at all. Hollywood, he'd tell me, was where stars were made.

Listening to Dad talk, things ceased to take on the life or death proportions Mom assigned everything. Mountains were downsized to their appropriate molehill stature, and it became clear to me that it wasn't up to me to make the world smile. Dad was big enough and bright enough to amuse us all for ages to come. I would laugh so hard I'd produce tears, and I knew that he loved me, even though he never said so, and that even though he never called, he was thinking about me, saving up his stories for me to make me laugh.

After lunch, we made a few more rounds before heading up the Grapevine. I gave Hollywood one long last look before it completely disappeared behind the hills, imagining that the stars above Hollywood were brighter than the ones back at home because this was where they were made. Sometimes now, when the buildings and cars sparkle in the darkness, I think, maybe there was some truth, after all, to my childhood fantasies.

A few hours later, made regrettably shorter by sleep,

Dad deposited me in front of Mom's apartment. It would be years before I'd hear from him again, years before I knew that there were footprints in front of the Chinese theater, or that other people's idea of sight-seeing involved actually stopping the car and getting out, walking around, with that special someone, doing ridiculously stupid things you could get away with because you were tourists, and years before I knew the word 'good-bye' didn't always have a depressing connotation of permanence.

Still, person, place, or thing, whatever Hollywood was or is, the fact is, when I was finally able to move out of Mom's life, I chose to start mine right there, not as a dreamer, not as a fortune-seeker, more of an observer than anything else.

That was the summer I was twenty-one, the year that— if you believed everything Old Blue Eyes crooned and for some reason I wanted to—was supposed to be a very good year. I'm sure it was somewhere, for someone, but for me it was a year like any other.

I found an apartment, a job in a production office, and started to carve out my life, mainly by removing unwanted items, like bad memories. On Mondays after work I'd go out drinking with some of the girls who were jaded from working in television too long. I would go because my only other offer was my couch and another evening of reality TV. Nothing ever came of it, though. I didn't have much in common with them, and I was too lazy to work at friendships.

I'd spend my weekends at a coffeehouse on Melrose and

fritter the day away, sipping coffee, occasionally nibbling a muffin, watching the beautiful people, who would bring their laptops to work on their latest screenplay, or dog-eared scripts to study lines for the play they were understudying. Most, I imagined, were out-of-work actors or models, content to spend their days lounging at the coffeehouse, doing nothing but wait for their big break. I admired their ability to maintain their faith and devotion, to continue to worship at the altar of shattered hopes and dreams, while I rapidly descended into the abyss of disbelief.

I would alternate between watching them, sipping my coffee, and contemplating the palm trees, tall and stately, wavering in the breeze, like idle thoughts. I'd remember how one of the characters in *The Way We Were* said that even the palm trees were transplants. That didn't sound true—they looked so native. But, if they were transplants, maybe there was hope for me.

Sometimes I really did feel like Hollywood was home, and that I'd settled here to wait for Dad, because I instinctively knew he'd return here, as if he and I were characters in a World War II film who got separated by circumstances and agreed to meet in LA if one of us escaped or survived the prison camp. So, I spent my days working, my weekends at the coffeehouse, waiting.

I spent Labor Day at the coffeehouse that year. Technically, it wasn't a weekend, but I wasn't working and had no place else to go. The aluminum chairs outside the coffeehouse and the glass building across the street seemed to trap and reflect the already glaring sunlight. In addition to making it feel at least ten percent warmer than the forecast, it made everything around appear to glow, as if we were living in a post-modern sci-fi world where life was permanently tinged in metallic gray.

I was sitting alone at a table, drinking a latte, and feeling incredibly friendless, regretting that fact that it was the last of the dog days of summer, and I hadn't been to the beach once, when a voice asked:

"Is this seat taken?"

I looked up. Standing in the glare of the autumnal sun was George, a guy from work.

He was the guy all the women at work made a fuss over, tall, with standard good looks, so much so, he was almost a cliché. I was bound and determined to ignore his existence, mainly because he seemed bent on ignoring mine.

"No," I said, so lost in my thoughts that my voice hadn't found its way out.

"I'm sorry," he said, looking down at me, smiling as if he knew a secret joke that he planned on keeping to himself.

"It's not taken," I said, moving my purse and pushing the chair towards him with my foot.

He took the chair and sat down. "It's pretty crowded today. I hope you don't mind."

I shook my head, turning my attention back to the palm trees.

"Cool." He took the lid off his coffee cup and began pouring bag after bag of sugar into it, stirring with great intensity.

"I know it's a pretty old joke, but would you like some coffee with that?"

"Hum?" He looked confused, as if surprised I was still there. "Coffee with that? Oh, yeah. I guess I overdid it a bit, huh?"

"No. I'm just a one bag per cup, myself."

"You're a tough chick. Or if that's not PC, a strong woman."

I shrugged. "Maybe."

"So...I'm gonna grab a bagel. Watch my cup, will you?"

When he returned he said, "So, Jessica, you know, the funny thing is...I always thought you were stuck up. You never talk to me."

I wanted to tell him that I had just been reflecting on my misconceptions of him, but settled for the noncommittal: "I guess I just don't make friends easily."

"You're not from around here?" he said. It was more of a statement than a question.

"Not really. I'm from up north."

"San Francisco?"

"Sort of."

"I can relate. I grew up back east. And LA's different. I mean, I've gotten a lot dumber since I moved here."

I laughed the way you do when it's expected.

"But seriously," he continued, "have you noticed that you're losing gray matter? I think it's something to do with the sun. Or maybe it's global warming. I think it's safe to blame everything on global warming."

I laughed and told him I thought it was just a myth.

"No," he said, smiling. "Global warming is a certifiable fact." He feigned shock. "Wait a minute. Don't tell me... you're a Republican?"

"I mean, people in Los Angeles just seem dumber. They're shallow everywhere. The people here just don't try to hide it. They honor it. They celebrate superficiality."

"I think you may be on to something," he said.

I studied him carefully. Maybe the women at work were right, he was nice-looking. But I was pretty, too. At least, that's what Mom always used to tell me, because I looked so much like her.

He laughed a lot at what I said, and I was incredibly witty that day. There was something about the stifling heat, caffeine, and his smile that proved to be a lethal combination.

We talked about this and that, like what had been our favorite show in fifth grade, and what was our all-time favorite movie. He groaned when I said, *Breakfast at Tiffany's* and I said, "Typical," when he said, *Star Wars*.

Finally, we got around to our families. He was the second of three brothers. His parents were in "the business," which is why he ended up in "the business." They nagged him because he drove too fast and drank too much, but deep down they were proud of him, because he was kind to dogs and the elderly.

"Sounds nice," I said. "I'm an only child." I figured if I volunteered information, I could control the flow. I didn't want to open the door to questions about my family, which could only be answered by telling him how Mom wandered from place to place, forcing me to follow her on her ridiculously impossible quest for happiness; how my memories of my Dad were dominated by our one-time trip to Hollywood; how I'd moved to Hollywood because it made me think of the one time in my life I'd been happy; how I think about Dad all of the time, trying to imagine what he's doing in Mexico—sometimes it seems he must be rotting away in a Mexican prison, the way tough guys did in the movies, but mostly, I imagine that he's somewhere living happily ever after without me; how the beauty of that day is constantly in danger of being overshadowed by the thought that maybe Dad has forgotten about it, so maybe it never happened.

"Were you ever lonely?" he asked.

"Not until I moved here," I said, without thinking.

Lunchtime came and went, and neither of us was in the mood to go home. George went in for a ridiculously over-priced salad, which we split, and later I got us refills on our drinks. Then, around dinnertime, he asked if I lived nearby. After determining that we lived within blocks of one another, we decided to walk home together.

The sun was hitting the mountains, making everything look golden, magical, and Hollywood, as if we were all players on a soundstage. Even the future looked brighter, so I ignored the nagging voice in my head that was doing its best to remind me that it was simply an illusion.

As we approached my street, we passed an all-natural gourmet frozen yogurt shop and George stopped to look inside, like a kid in front of a pet store.

"Have you ever been here?" he asked.

"Nope," I told him.

"How could you live so close, and not go in? Jeez Louise!" He grabbed my hand and pulled me inside, saying: "It's too hot to say no to ice cream!"

We ordered fanciful concoctions like peanut butter caramel crunch and wild raspberry chocolate swirl cheesecake.

George held out a spoonful. "Try this. The best you've ever tasted, right?"

I nodded, smiling, as we stepped back outside where the flower shop next door was blaring big band music.

George grabbed my frozen yogurt and set it on the stoop.

"Come on, Jess, let's dance."

"Here?" I hesitated.

"Of course."

I looked at him. His foot was keeping time and I could tell that his offer was fleeting. A moment later, he would discover that I wasn't what I was pretending to be. The golden spell cast by the sun would be broken, he would see that I was disappointingly ordinary, and he would leave.

So I danced with him. It was exactly the sort of thing you'd see in a black and white movie starring someone like Claudette Colbert. A silver roadster drove by and the driver honked at us while the passenger gave us two thumbs up.

We walked home slowly, like a southern drawl, as if doing so would make the day last forever. Every now and then he'd lean down to point something out, and he'd stumble into me, catching me as we laughed. Eventually we stopped in front of my apartment.

"So, this is it?" he asked.

"Thanks." I got my key out and unlocked the door. I didn't want to go inside. I didn't want to say goodbye to George.

"It was a perfect day," he said. Then, leaning down one last time, he quickly kissed me. When I went inside, I remembered that he hadn't said 'See you tomorrow,' 'See you around,' or anything else, for that matter.

The next day we went back to work and back to ignoring each other. Sometimes I'd catch a glimpse of him or hear his voice in the hallway and wonder if that day had ever happened.

Autumn panted along. Winter blew in on the Santa Anas. Then one day I got a package. George brought it in and dropped it on my desk.

"Hey, there," he said awkwardly. I didn't know why I should be angry with him. He never said he'd call. He hadn't broken any promises to me. According to the rumor mill, he was seeing someone. No one thought to link his name with mine, and if I hadn't still remembered his kiss, I wouldn't have either.

George lingered. "Who's it from?"

I looked at the package, a small, plain box wrapped in brown paper with my name and address scrawled in thin, vapid writing. The postmark was from Arizona, and I didn't know anyone in Arizona.

"I don't know," I said, shaking the box.

"Sounds expensive," George joked. "Open it. I'll wait."

I opened the box, trying to ward off the persistent ominous sensation its arrival had triggered.

Inside was a note from a woman claiming to be my father's girlfriend, and a bundle of letters. He had died, she wrote, and she'd found the letters with his things. Since they were mine, she wondered if I'd want them back.

I looked at them. They were all the letters I'd written him over the years, written in childish handwriting that I barely recognized, and there were snapshots I'd sent him, as well as formal portraits from school, smiling at him through camera, year after year. The pictures were all signed. "To Dad, from Jessica. I love you very much," they said. Sometimes I'd written, "I miss you" or "Write soon." I remembered some of the letters, but I mainly remembered the disappointment.

"Those are a lot of letters," George said.

I looked up at him. "I didn't know he was in Arizona," I said. "I didn't know he had a girlfriend."

"I gotta go, Jess," he said. "But don't worry. We'll get together tomorrow."

George left, and I collected the letters and put them in my purse. I didn't know anything about my dad, except that he had kept the letters, all those letters he'd never answered.

I met George at the coffeehouse the next morning. "Hey," he said as I walked up, "I saved you a seat."

He split his muffin with me as I told him the story of my trip to Hollywood with Dad.

"Well," he said, "that settles it. We're going to have a day today. Hollywood and Highland, the Wax Museum, the Walk of Fame, hot dogs at Pink's, the works."

Nightfall came and we found ourselves eating Thai food on Sunset. "Asian Elvis" was singing *You Don't Know Me* in broken English when George reached over the table to touch my hand.

"Ready?"

We walked out onto the sidewalk. It was nearly dark, but still warm. The street was as busy as it had been at noon and showed no sign of slowing down. We crossed the street amid honking horns and screeching brakes.

I shivered.

"Cold?" George asked.

"No," I said.

He took my hand and led me down the street, past the hookers and the pushers who seemed oblivious to our presence, as if we existed on two separate and distinct planes. He paused in front of an apartment building. "I think this is the one," he said, looking up.

We went inside and took the elevator up.

The elevator opened to the roof, and George stepped out, leading me by the hand. "Take a look," he said, "beautiful, isn't it?"

I looked down on the street. From our height we could see a steady stream of cars, lights, but no people. Behind us was the Hollywood sign, somehow still visible in the dark, as if it was a hologram permanently etched on my consciousness.

"I wish I'd told him one last time that I loved him, that I'd forgiven him for leaving me and never thinking about me."

"He thought about you, Jess."

"Well, I couldn't feel it. Just like he couldn't feel that I loved him."

"But he knew, Jess. They always know. And it kills them, because they know they don't deserve it."

I held back a sob.

He nudged me. "Let him go, Jess. Let him go here."

"What?"

"The letters, Jess. You have to let go."

I took the letters out of my purse, and we ripped them up. Then George helped me throw them over the side of the building. I watched as they serenely floated down, like confetti on New Year's Eve.

I cried silently.

George held me, brushing the wet hair from my face.

"You love it here, Jess. Cheap and ugly as it is, it was the one place you felt happy."

I knew he was right. Places or ideas or people didn't have to be perfect to be beautiful.

George took my hand and, as we watched the bits of paper drift down on the street below, I suddenly felt calm.

Night settled over Hollywood. George held me. Somewhere below, a homeless man carried on an angry one-sided conversation.

BLUE LIGHTS

The lights at the airport glowed blue at night. I looked for them on trips home from Grandma's house, anxiously waiting until we were close enough to see the lights, calm and blue in the pitch darkness, lighting the way, because even when I was sure of nothing else, I knew the lights meant we were home.

Mom would plow along, silently. She never talked to me then. I might ask questions that she'd have to answer—like what had happened to Joey, why they'd sent him away, and was he ever coming back.

Instead, I'd listen to the rhythm of the road and watch for the reliable milestones that told me where we were. Sometimes, I'd study Mom's face, so beautiful and ageless in the dark, and think how much we really did look alike, how in the quiet darkness, it was as if she and I were suspended in time.

Once we came home in the morning, and to my chagrin, I discovered in the daylight, the airport didn't have the same magic; the blue lights disappeared, and the runway, which in the dark seemed limitless, did not stretch into infinity after all, but was only faded asphalt edged with weeds and dead grass.

They closed the airport the year I started ninth grade. The city had voted to build a bigger airport farther from the center of town, and little by little the old airport began to die. Weeds overtook what used to be the runway, and eventually the blue lights faded from view.

From my window on the plane, I could see what looked like perfectly grid neighborhoods, angular streets, kidney-shaped swimming pools, street lamps, trees, closer and closer until we passed the edge of town, racing first towards a dark field, then asphalt, and finally the sea of blue lights. Our rude landing ended my daydream, reminding me that this must be what being born feels like. Now I had to face Mom, ready or not.

The death had been unexpected. Mom called me at work the day before with the news. I immediately called Troy to ask if he'd drive me to the airport.

"I have a meeting," he said, sounding harried.

I waited, expecting him to say, 'But I'll cancel. What time do you have to be there?' When he didn't, I said, "Then I'll take a cab. Or I'll park my car there. Never mind, I'll figure it out."

"Hold on," he said, "let me think." I could hear someone speaking to him in the background. "Babe, can I call you in a sec?"

"Forget it," I said, hanging up. I wanted him to drop

everything. 'I'll go with you,' I wanted him to say. 'It's going to be all right. And one day you won't miss her so much.' But he had a meeting, and I took a cab.

The clouds we'd flown through gave way to a light drizzle. Mom was waiting for me outside with an umbrella. As I hugged her, I lamented the years I'd let slip by in endless meetings and impossible deadlines, leaving me so exhausted, and Mom so frail.

"It happened so fast—in her sleep, just the way she wanted," Mom said, and because I didn't answer, she added, "She wasn't in any pain."

Looking into Mom's eyes I could see the emptiness I felt where I imagined my heart would be. People would talk about visiting, calling, and buying gifts for their grandparents, but I knew, from here on out, it was just Mom and me.

As we walked to the parking lot, Mom did her best to shield me with her umbrella while grilling me about work, Troy, and my new apartment. I answered dutifully, thankful for the raindrops that hid my tears.

True to our tradition, we didn't talk during the ride from the airport. In my absence, the town had been built up beyond recognition. I watched Mom navigate her way through streets I didn't remember, making turns I could somehow predict, weaving intricate patterns in a labyrinth that led home. Everything looked damp as if it was covered in years of moss. I wondered if it had always looked that way and I'd somehow failed to notice.

I knew Mom had been hoping we could talk, but as soon

as we got home, I told her I was beat, and could we please catch up in the morning. She looked at me with pleading eyes, and even though I could tell she wanted to talk about Grandma, or ask me more questions about Troy, she let me retire without protest. Once in my old room, I went straight to bed, without bothering to change clothes, or even to get under the covers.

When I awoke, it was nearly 11:30 and, although the rain had stopped, the day looked cheerless.

"Do you want to see Joey?" Mom asked as soon as she saw me.

I poured a cup of coffee and sat at the table.

"You hungry?" she asked.

"A little," I said.

She set an omelet down in front of me.

"How is he?" I asked.

"Fine. He never changes. We'll die, but Joey will always be Joey." Her voice was flat and as dull as it was outside.

"He doesn't know," Mom said. "I thought it would be better coming from you. He listens to you."

Growing up, Joey and I shared everything, including a birth date. We were close, and trying to live without him was like looking into a mirror and no longer being able to see your own reflection staring back.

We'd always had a special connection, Joey and I. I used to think I understood him and he understood me. Later, when we found out he was sick, it felt like everything I'd ever known had been a miserable lie.

Mom used to say I never see people the way they really are, that when I really love someone I go blind and deaf, and for years I'd convinced myself that the doctors were all wrong about Joey. He'd come home, somehow the void created by the years we'd spent apart would be filled, and I'd be whole again.

But that was life. Joey went away and I grew up alone.

I remember when he started changing, although, looking back, there were always hints that he was different. He always seemed to know things, dark and deep secrets that he was unable to share. I could always tell, though, that there was something going on behind those liquid eyes of his that was far more interesting than what was going on between us. And one day, the eerie sounds coming from his room late at night became too much, and he had to go away.

A solemn nurse led us down a long, dim, pale green hall that smelled of canned vegetables and antiseptic, past open doors revealing patients engaged in various social activities, but each in his own world. She stopped outside Joey's room, and rapped disinterestedly on the door.

He was sitting on his bed, facing away from us, and although his curtain was open and he was looking towards the window, there was something about his still posture that told me he didn't see what was out there.

He turned slowly, and seeing us, he stood.

"Well, hello," he said. His voice sounded rehearsed and

formal.

"Joey," I went to hug him. He stepped back slightly, but allowed me to put my arms around him.

He was wearing a thin cotton bathrobe over his pajamas, and I realized that I expected to see him in flannel, because in all my daydreams he is always wearing flannel and looks warm and cared-for, as if they had been healing him all of these years instead of merely maintaining him. The real-life Joey looked thin and old and diminished. He held his mouth as if he was unsure of the security of his teeth, his mouth forever forming words he will never utter. My throat tightened as I reflected on what a shame it was that we were constantly disappointing one another, but only because we are always hoping the best for those we love.

He was standing, holding one leg in front of the other, a position that forced his body to tilt unnaturally and teeter forward. It must be difficult to balance that way, I thought, because I didn't want to think of anything else, like how he was doing. But Joey, in his ratty old bathrobe, seemed accustomed to this posture.

Only his eyes were as I remembered, magnificent, and young, the way they were the day he left. The eyes never change, only the view. He proudly showed me his ceramics, happy with the present; not at all curious about what's going on inside me, as I am about him.

Mom's expression took on that pained look of one who has suffered much. As usual, this was happening to her. She left, saying she was going to hunt down some coffee.

Joey retreated back into himself, possibly sensing my lack of interest in his vase.

I sat next to him on his bed and told him about Grandma.

"I've heard similar rumors before," he said cryptically. "But I never believe them."

I looked at him, thinking how it's a pity I can't fix him but, then, I can't even fix myself.

I once had a boyfriend who used to say, "You remind me of an injured bird. I want to fix your broken wings so you can fly again." In all fairness to him, it was the 80s and I did go around wearing a tragic expression and dark eye makeup. Never mind that he was butchering the lyrics of a song, the idea of one person fixing another person appealed to me back then.

Now I realize that no one has ever had much success in putting someone back together and restoring him to the way he was before. I've decided that your best bet is trying to make it through life without too much damage in the first place.

Joey and I went to the cafeteria. He selected his food according to some highly developed codified system that I couldn't figure out, and we sat down to eat.

"Does it seem to you that everything in this place is painted pale green?" I asked, picking at a questionable substance on my plate.

"I like green," he said calmly.

I let him eat a few more bites before resuming the conversation.

"Joey, I just want to make sure you understand. Grandma's not coming back. She won't call anymore. She can't come to see you."

"I understand," Joey said. His face was calm.

"Are you sad?" I asked.

"I believe I am," he answered, but he seemed more interested in finishing his gelatin.

Mom returned with Joey's doctor, who nodded to Joey and me before continuing across the cafeteria.

"Joseph," she said, "we've got to go now. Say good-bye to your sister." She kissed Joey, and he stood still as I approached him for a hug.

This time when I hugged him, he did wrap his arms around me, though he didn't squeeze me like Troy does. It was the best he could do, and it wasn't fair of me to expect more.

Mom and I walked out together. I looked back several times to see if Joey was still watching us from the pale green hallway. Mom kept looking straight ahead, making quick, sharp footsteps on the sleek cold floor. I've never understood their relationship, but I suppose you have to be inside a relationship to make sense of it.

We drove home in silence. I wondered what Mom had talked to Joey's doctor about since we'd given up asking about his progress long ago. Joey had been one thing; he became something else. There was nothing for us to do but accept it.

As we drove, I noticed what appeared to be jewel-encrusted hills to our left. The closer we got, the less the colors looked like jewels, turning mundanely into headlights and streetlights, until I couldn't see them at all, and I knew we had become just another light.

Later, over dinner, Mom told me she's been looking into options about what to do with Joey when she dies. "You won't want him," she said. "You and Troy will want a family."

I wanted to tell her that whether or not Troy and I want a family, Joey is my family and you can't just throw people away, but I thought of Joey sitting there eating his gelatin while someone tries to explain to him that I have died, and I couldn't get my mouth to form the words.

Troy called later that evening to say that he was flying in for the funeral. "My flight arrives at 5:45 in the morning. Ungodly, right? Pick me up, will you? I've never been to your Mom's and you know me and directions, I'll end up south of the border." He laughed brightly, but I could hear the question mark in his voice.

"Thanks, Honey," I said.

"Okay," he said, sounding relieved. "See you tomorrow."

I borrowed Mom's car and left first thing the next morning. Somehow, despite having been half-asleep on the ride from the airport, I was able to find my way back without getting lost.

Troy was one of the last to exit. He looked as if he needed a haircut, though it had only been days since I'd seen him.

His sleepy eyes lit up when he saw me and crinkled as they always did when he smiled at me. Catching me up in a big hug, he said: "I missed you, Beautiful." He handed me his computer while he adjusted his carryon.

"So, why'd you come? I told you not to worry."

"And you didn't mean it."

"I did..."

"Hey, I know you, remember? Besides, I remember when my Grandmother died. It would've helped if you'd been there."

"You were thirteen. We didn't even know each other then."

"Pity," he said, smiling, and I remembered why, as infuriating as I sometimes found him, I could never hold anything against him.

He took my hand. I let him see my tears, and I could tell that he was sad for me. He wanted to fix it, but knew he was powerless and knowing that he wanted to was enough.

One day he'd cry at my funeral, or maybe, I'd cry at his. In the meantime, he'd be there, like a blue light, pointing the way home.

SUMMER FLIES

The summer flies were starting to die. I sat on the porch swing, bathing in the friendly sunlight, happy for no particular reason, listlessly swatting at them as they buzzed around my face in near slow motion. Earlier in the summer, when the flies were still capable of nimble acrobatics, I made it my business to kill as many as I could. Now I watched them with exaggerated forbearance, consoling myself with the notion that, come spring, they'd be back.

Soon Mom would come out to check on me. She hadn't let me alone since we arrived at the farm a few days ago.

"Deannie, you okay?" "You want some more lemonade?" "Can I get you some pie?"

"I'm fine, Mom," I would say. She couldn't understand that I wasn't a baby anymore.

Whenever I'd venture into the house, Mom and Grandma would lower their voices. I'd get a piece of pie or lemonade or whatever I'd come for. "How's Grandpa?" I'd ask, but Mom and Grandma would only exchange knowing looks and tell me to go outside and swing.

I'd hurry back outside to the bright sunlight, so different

from the dark, somber house, careful not to let the screen door slam on my way out.

In the evenings Dad would call from the city and ask to speak to me. I would take the phone from Grandma, feeling very grown up as I told him how big the baby chicks were getting and how I had discovered mint growing outside next to the water faucet.

When I asked him if he wanted to speak to Mom, he would say it was late, he was sure she was tired, and he would speak to her in the morning.

Sometimes, at night, I'd wake up to the sound of voices downstairs. Listening carefully, I could make out Mom and Grandma talking in hushed voices.

Their voice rose and fell, like music, steady and progressive. Their conspiratorial nature left me feeling angry and defiant.

Sneaking down to the landing, I stuck my head through the banister, and as I leaned forward, I could see Mom sitting in Grandpa's favorite chair. An empty bottle and a glass were on the table beside her, as Grandma stood over her, looking at her the way Mom looked at me when I refused to pick up after myself.

"...don't understand how this could happen. How could he do this to me...and to Deannie? She adores him," Mom was saying.

"Think of Deannie," Grandma said. "She needs you."

I went back to my room and climbed back into bed. I tried to fall asleep, but my room seemed dark and large, and monsters were certain to be lurking about, since Mom hadn't tucked me in that night. I huddled under my quilt, feeling alone and small, until it was so unbearable that I jumped up and threw the door open. Looking down the hallway, I could see a faint light bleeding out from under the door of Grandpa's room. There would be no monsters in there with him.

I liked my Grandpa, although I hadn't seen much of him on this visit. He was a grave, quiet man who allowed me to follow him around the farm while he did his work. He never made me feel like I was in the way, or too little, or too much of a girl. He didn't say much, Grandma did the talking for the two of them, but I sensed that being a part of him somehow made me significant.

I opened the door and tiptoed in. Grandpa was resting in a big hospital bed, breathing heavily. The light from a fluorescent lamp flickered dimly in the corner, creating strange angular shadows on the walls and floor. I crept up to him and took his hand.

He raised his head to look at me with slow, lethargic movements. Instead of smiling, like he usually did when he saw me, he painstakingly closed his eyes and opened them again.

"I would have come sooner," I told him, "but they wouldn't let me."

"I've been thinking about you, Deannie," he whispered.

I found a chair and pulled it close so I could climb into bed with him, and slept there till morning.

After that, whenever I woke up at night, I would sneak down the hall to Grandpa's room. I'd sit in the rocker and watch him sleep, comforted by the sound of his labored breathing.

One morning, I didn't wake up in time to sneak back into my room, and Grandma caught me.

"What's Deannie doing in here?" she called to my Mom and they both shooed me out.

"You know better than that," they told me, shaking their heads disapprovingly.

I went outside and found the dog sleeping in the grass. I sat down beside him and laughed aloud as his back twitched involuntarily whenever the flies buzzed around him.

Lying back on the grass, I watched the sky, which was perfectly blue, except for one fluffy cloud floating overhead. When I closed my eyes, I could feel the sun, so warm I could almost see it.

After a while, the dog jumped up and ran off, chasing an imaginary rabbit he must have been dreaming about. When his animated barking died down, I could hear a faint sound, almost a whimper coming from the house.

Wondering if the dog had in fact caught a small animal, I decided to follow the sound. Reaching the porch, I found Mom sitting there, crying. Silently, I went to her and sat down, snuggling my head on her arm. She grabbed me and hugged me until I almost couldn't breathe.

"He's gone," she said. "Grandpa's gone."

Mom started to wail like a dying animal, and I wailed with her, not wanting to let her cry alone.

My stomach felt uneasy, but I clung tightly to Mom and cried my eyes out. I cried for Grandpa. I cried because they hadn't told me he was dying. But mostly, I cried because I was too young, and he was too old. Grandpa had slowed down for good, and was never coming back, no matter how many springs came and went.

We didn't go back home at the end of summer. Dad sent our things up to Grandma's, and when September came I started school. Finally, when she thought I could handle it, Mom told me what I seemed to already know: that she and Dad were getting a divorce.

Sometimes, late in summer when the flies start to die, I remember sitting on Grandma's porch and wonder at the innocence of the girl who sat there swinging lazily in the summer breeze, and I am filled with the same confused pity I felt for the summer flies.

THE WEDDING DRESS

Angela got dressed and went to work as she always did. She wore the peacock blue silk blouse with the Kelly green plaid skirt. Loud, perhaps, but something had to counter the relentless June gloom that had settled in overnight.

Turning her key in the lock, she tried to forget the off-white linen envelope sitting on the side table, mocking her with its contents.

At lunch, she chose the tuna salad instead of the chicken, for no particular reason, and listened as Nancy recounted her previous night's exploits, interjecting what she hoped were suitably wide-eyed "You didn'ts!" and "You dids," between Nancy's fantastical tale which, she wasn't sure but, sounded vaguely like something she'd read in a back-issue of Cosmo while waiting for Mr. George to cut her hair last weekend. Nancy, she knew, was potty-training her three-year-old.

Angela went back to work, but found herself staring into space, wondering when Thomas would return her call, pondering when life had lost its element of surprise, finally realizing it must have been around the time her parents had gathered her and her older brother around the perfectly polished dining room table to inform them of their impending divorce.

"But they seemed so happy," she'd cried to her brother years later.

"No," he'd told her. "They seemed married."

She hadn't known what he meant at the time. But lately, whenever Thomas called, she'd had a glimmer.

The call came around five minutes to six.

"So, the wedding's this Saturday? Angela, I wish you'd given me more notice. I'm working on this project, and I just can't," Thomas said. There was noise and confusion in the background, which almost tricked Angela into thinking that Thomas worked in a bustling office with plenty to do, instead of the nearly catatonic mortgage company.

"Well," Angela began, looking at the clock. It would be six in a minute. Time to go home. "Well, I'd forgotten about it until I found the invitation this morning. It just sort of snuck up on me. Anyway, it's addressed to Angela Hill and guest." When Thomas didn't volunteer a response, Angela added, "And, I figured, since you were my boyfriend, you'd want to go." She tried to make her voice as coy as possible, but realized she only succeeded in sounding ridiculous, as if she was still in junior high. But after all, what did you call someone who bought you expensive dinners at the Grove, and ordered your drinks just the way you liked them, and bragged to his friends about you in glowing tones? Thomas did have his faults, but he was comforting to have around.

"It's not that I don't want to go," Thomas said, putting conspicuous emphasis on the word, 'want.' "I just can't, Ang. I'm really, really sorry. Good-bye, Love."

Angela hung up, still smarting from what she considered two too many 'reallys' for a sincere apology. She briefly considered going solo and telling everyone that her husband would have come, had he not been stationed "over there." That would be sure to elicit several sympathetic, knowing looks.

Angela tossed her cell phone into her Kate Spade knock-off and headed for the parking lot.

After arriving home, she decided to call Nancy to attempt to cajole her into going.

"I'd love to go, Angie. You know me—I'm not one to turn down free food, but I've got nothing to wear."

"Sure you do. What about that black dress I helped you pick out for Ryan's office party last year?"

"That was 10 pounds ago. You know, Angie, not everyone has your discipline."

Angela begged and pleaded and reminded Nancy about the time she'd put the leather peacoat that Nancy had to have on her American Express because Ryan had put a moratorium on purchasing nonessential items. Finally, Nancy relented and agreed that if she could squeeze into the black dress, she'd go.

Angela arrived at Nancy's house with several pairs of Spanx, a sewing kit, and a box of laxatives—just in case—and the two women went to work.

Several hours later, Nancy was still not in the dress, and Angela was starting to question her level of commitment to their friendship. If Nancy couldn't do this one thing for her, really, what was the point?

"It's hopeless," Nancy said. "It doesn't fit. I should have taken it to Goodwill months ago." Angela looked skeptical, but only said, "If it doesn't fit, it doesn't fit." And Nancy added, "I don't get why this wedding is such a big deal, anyway. He's just your ex."

"That's because you don't have any exes," Angela told her accusingly. "You married your only."

The rest of the week passed quickly. By Saturday, the June gloom had lifted, revealing the perfect spring weather that had been hiding all along.

Angela slipped on her dress and, after downing a preliminary glass of Chardonnay, left for the country club.

The gardens outside the club had never looked lovelier. White folding chairs were laid out in a perfect grid. Elegant ladies in pastel hats peppered the lawn like spring flowers. Debonair men in penguin suits stood stiffly to the side, staring wistfully at the green in the distance. Everything looked festive and floral. Bucolic, was the word, Angela thought. It always sounded to her like an illness, but was the perfect word for a quaint, lovely, suburban setting like this.

And there was David, standing before God and everyone, looking nervous as he kept wiping imaginary beads of sweat from his supercilious brow. Angela didn't want to be critical, but she couldn't help but notice that over the years he'd gotten downright chubby.

The music reached a crescendo, and amid the "oohs" and "ahhs" of the audience, the bride began her tentative walk down the aisle. Angela was more than a little pleased to note that the bride looked somewhat drab, even in her designer dress, and, not to brag, but in her apricot tulle and lace garden dress and antique jade velvet jacket, Angela was looking positively radiant.

At dinner Angela found herself seated at a table with several middle-aged spinster aunts and David's cousin, a miniature Bill Gates, who kept suggestively raising a glass of 7-up at her. Just before coffee was served, David stopped by to thank the table for troubling themselves to come.

"Angela," he said, feigning shock, and Angela remembered he'd always been unctuous to the point of nausea, "it's so good to see you."

"Likewise," she said. "I was thrilled to hear you'd found someone."

"Isn't she lovely?" he said, his eyes beaming with pride at his bride.

"*My Cherie Amour,*" Angela felt like answering, since apparently, they were reduced to quoting Stevie Wonder song titles. Instead, she said in her most condescending voice, "We're so happy for you both."

Dave scanned the table. "Oh, is he here, your other half? I'd heard you were seeing someone."

"No," Angela said simply. She gave Dave her tolerant look, and forced a smile.

Dave smiled back. "Would you like to dance, for old times' sake?" he asked suddenly.

I'll Always Love You by Taylor Dane was playing on the sound system. Dave led Angela to the floor, and was it her imagination, or was that a look of part longing, part remorse playing on his face?

Smiling, Angela thought to herself that attending Dave's wedding by herself was not the absolute tragedy she'd thought it would be.

TOO MANY PEOPLE

"Too many people."

I'd known Conchita ten years and that was the first time I'd ever heard her say that phrase correctly. No matter how many times I tried to explain when to use "many" and when to use "much," she was constantly mixing them up. I finally decided it was one of those things you just had to know, because it sounded right.

Apparently it all sounded right to Conchita, so she would say "Too much people," if we were standing in line, or "Too much cars" if we were stuck on the freeway.

It was kind of weird, because apart from this mental block, Conchita had a pretty good grasp of English. It was practically her first language, because she'd been speaking it since she started pre-school. Stranger still, was the fact that she had a heavy accent, which I noticed immediately the first time we met in eighth grade.

"Where're you from?" I remember asking.

"Cuba." She seemed offended.

Later I found out that she thought she spoke English

without an accent. "*Ju shad hair ma mom. Hair accen' is so theek.*"

Lord only knows why it took her at least ten years to master this relatively simple concept. But, we were standing in line at the bank on this particular day, and she happened to be right on two counts—there were too many people.

That was the summer disappointment came to rest on my shoulders, probably because I'd been standing in one place too long. I was disappointed because after breaking up with me because he needed "space," Dirk was moving in with some girl named Janet he'd met at the gym, and I realized that I couldn't be everything to him as, pathetically, for almost ten years he had been for me.

I was disappointed because I had been in Hollywood for three whole years and the only thing I had to show for it was a futon in Conchita's living room and one half of a 1985 Honda Accord. Mainly the passenger side because Conchita insisted on doing all of the driving, barreling down one narrow Hollywood back street after the other, apparently afraid that if she didn't get wherever it was she was going as quickly as possible, she would miss out on something.

I was disappointed because I finally realized that the downside of being popular in high school is that, for the majority of people who didn't actually go to high school with you, it doesn't matter that you were once on top. Everyone starts at 'go' in the real world, and you don't get brownie points for once-upon-a-time being the envy of all the overweight sixteen-year-old girls in your hometown.

As frightening a thought as it was, I was starting to realize that I had never been anyone's favorite, and I was starting to suspect that, maybe, underneath all the Maybelline, I was average.

This thought, which woke me at night and would creep into my head whenever I had a spare, lonely moment, first came to me at an audition.

My agent had called me that morning, sort of last minute, telling me about a casting call for a new cop drama, an unglamorous guest spot—a drug addicted prostitute suspected of that week's murder. Having nothing else to do, and a superstitious inability to say no to my agent, I took a shower and went down to the casting office.

I'd gotten to the point where I no longer looked around when entering casting offices. They always looked the same: worn industrial carpet, cracked vinyl chairs, used couches that had seen better days, aluminum side tables with dog eared, marked up copies of scripts. Instead, I'd walk in, find the spot that was farthest away from other people, and wait until I was called in.

"What have you been in?" The voice was lilting and light, in contrast to mine, which lately had been sounding heavy and dull to my ears.

I looked up. The fresh-faced actress who had been sitting on a chair on the other side of the room had joined me on the sofa. She was looking at me, smiling, questioning.

"I've done a few commercials. You?"

"Oh, my god. I used to do community theater back in

Omaha. I was Laurie in *Oklahoma!* I did a few plays in high school. But if I get this role, it'll be my first time doing TV. I'm so excited. Not that I hope that I get it and you don't. I'd be just as excited for you. I mean, someone has to get it. It might as well be you or me, right?"

She was oozing enthusiasm into the small waiting room, and frankly, I couldn't breathe. I wanted to tell her if that was how she really felt, she might as well go home, because second chances didn't come around that often in this town, so you'd better go for any chance you get. But I realized her words were probably just talk, so I nodded politely, and picked up a script, telling her I needed to go over the lines.

"Good idea," she said, apparently not offended by my lack of desire to converse with her. She picked up a script and began reading lines in an annoying stage whisper.

She got called in ahead of me, and I heard her gushing to the casting director about how excited and happy she was to be there, before the door closed behind her.

I went into the bathroom, fighting my way past the other actresses preening at the mirror. Since the lighting was much better than the lighting in our dank apartment, I could see the huge dark bags under my eyes, and the sickish tint my skin had taken on, and that, frankly, I was starting to look not so young. I considered putting on some more make-up, but decided there was no point.

When it was finally my turn to go in, I noticed right away that the casting director looked extremely familiar. I'd lived in Hollywood long enough to know that actors were as common as fitness clubs and Starbucks, that chances are that familiar-looking guy you ran into at Starbucks is not your distant cousin Joe, but the guy who played Burglar Number 3 in the movie you saw over the weekend. For some reason though I thought I really did know this woman, like she was my first grade teacher, or something.

"You look so familiar," I began.

"I guess I have one of those faces," she said, obviously ready to get down to business.

"Did you ever live in San Diego?"

"No," she said. I could tell she was starting to lose patience. "Which part are you reading for?"

I guess I kept staring at her, so she finally said, "I used to be famous."

"That's what it is. You were on *Night of a Thousand Laughs.* That was my favorite show when I was a kid. It killed me when they cancelled it."

"You and me both, kid. Now, are you here to audition, or what?"

"You're Clara Wallace! You were my favorite on the show. Everyone liked the guy. But I always thought you were funnier. I wanted to be just like you."

"Yeah, well, that was a long time ago," she said, but she was smiling now.

I read the lines, she made notes on her clipboard, and as I was leaving, she said, "It was nice meeting you. It's not every day I get recognized, by a young actress. Most of them think it all begins and ends with them."

I was sitting on the floor watching a TV show I'd auditioned for last month, when Conchita came home. "That role should have been yours, huh?" she said, opening a bag of chips.

"Oh well, you win some; you lose some."

"Yeah, if you have the stomach for it." Conchita laughed. "Maybe one day, huh? How'd it go today, anyway?"

"It was promising." I said.

"But, you think that every time, don't you? I guess Hollywood people are tricky. Big phonies, huh? They always make you think they like you, but then they choose someone else."

"That's life. Everyone gets to choose. There's no rhyme or reason to it. If they choose you, you win. If they don't choose you, they choose someone else. And one person's just as good as the next."

"You don't really believe that?" Conchita sounded shocked.

"After a few cattle calls, you would, too."

"That's too much depressing."

"That's life."

"Does this have anything to do with Dirk?"

"No," I said. "I'm past the stage in my life when everything goes back to Dirk."

"Because I thought maybe you were still mad about what happened between Dirk and me."

"Connie, I really don't want to talk about that."

Conchita was quiet for a few moments. Then, "He didn't

exactly choose me, either, you know," she said.

"We don't have Dirk in common. I was with him practically my whole adult life. It was my heart he ripped out and stomped on with combat boots. You had a few too many and kissed him once. It's not the same thing."

"He kissed me," she mumbled.

"Whatever. You and Dirk kissed. Can we please change the subject?"

Conchita looked mad, which irritated me.

"I got a raise today," she told me after a while.

"Another one?"

"Yes. My boss really likes me. He says I'm the best thing that ever happened to him. He's teaching me the business. Maybe one day he'll sell it to me. Imagine, little me—who didn't even go to college—a businesswoman. But my family has always had a head for business."

She'd told me her family history—wild and fanciful—once on a whale-watching field trip in tenth grade. All about how Castro had taken the family's millions, how they fled for their lives on a tiny raft, how they made their fortune back through shady business dealings and out-and-out cheating.

They'd gotten rich again, she assured me, until some rogue uncle met a Puerto Rican stripper from Brooklyn and together they fled the country with the family's millions.

Years later she told me she had made most of the story up, but I could never get her to tell me which parts, if any were true.

Several weeks passed, and I still hadn't heard anything

about the audition. Conchita would ask me about it every night, until finally, it seemed like she was mocking me. "They usually don't make you wait this long to find out if you got the part, or would you know about that?" she asked one evening.

So I decided, as uncomfortable as it might be, to call my agent the next day.

He wouldn't return my calls—either his snotty receptionist wouldn't give him the messages, or he'd finally given up on me—so I decided to call the casting office myself, anonymously, of course, because I needed an answer, even if it was the one I suspected it would be.

"Oh, we've cast the role already," Clara answered when, pretending to be an agent, I asked if I could schedule an appointment for my client to audition.

I was about to thank her and hang up, but she said, "Who is this, again?"

"Excuse me."

"You sound familiar. Haven't you auditioned for me? You're that girl, the one who used to watch *A Thousand Laughs*, aren't you?"

There was nothing for me to do but to own up to it.

"I thought I recognized your voice," she said. "I'll tell you what. Meet me at my office tomorrow. I'd like to see you again."

Before I had time to think what it could mean, I agreed to meet her the next day.

Clara couldn't see me when I got to her office. She was

on a conference call. So she had me wait outside her office with a bunch of child actors. I studied them, trying to decide who wanted it more, the kid or the parent. Sometimes it was obvious, but most of the time it was hard to tell. I found myself hating my mom for not dragging me to auditions when I was a kid.

After a while Clara came out of her office, and noticing me, she said, "Good, you made it. Come on in."

I followed her into her office, and instead of talking to me, she immediately got on the phone again, this time to someone who sounded like her kid because she kept saying things like, "Okay, so there's a roast in the fridge. Heat it up around five or so. I'll be home later tonight."

When she hung up, she looked at me. "I've brought you in to offer you a job."

"Great." After all, that was what I was there for. It didn't matter if it was the role I auditioned for or not. I'd finally be working as an actress, and that was all that counted.

"You can start as soon as you like. My assistant quit last week, and I'm desperate."

"So, is it for a TV show or a movie?"

Clara looked confused. "What are you talking about?"

"The role."

"Oh, you don't understand. I'm not offering you a part. I'm offering you a job. As my assistant."

"But, I'm not an assistant. I'm an actress."

Clara laughed. "That's exactly what I would have said when I was in my twenties. I wanted to be an actress, too.

Even worse, I wanted to be a star. I thought I had a pretty good shot at it, too. Little did I know."

"But, you were a star."

"Yeah, I was big once. Now, I cast for TV. Look, Kid, I like you, so I'm trying to help you out. It's never a bad idea to have something to fall back on."

"I'm sorry, Clara. I appreciate the offer. But this isn't what I want."

Clara looked at me for a long time. So long, I was beginning to feel uncomfortable. "Well, at least you know what you want. But what happens when your dream doesn't turn out the way you planned? Can you afford another one?"

I left her office and went to the nearest coffeehouse. As I sipped my latte, I kept trying to figure out if she was being sarcastic when she said that thing about me knowing what I wanted. I couldn't decide, and it really irritated me.

I didn't appreciate her questions, either. Didn't she know she was talking to the queen of disappointed dreams? Didn't she know I'd already decided to keep on pursuing impossible dreams—like the female Don Quixote of the new millennium—until I was as jaded and as cynical as possible? I mean, really, what other choice was there?

I'd decided long ago that there were only two kinds of people in the world: regular people and special people. I was special because I didn't want to be regular. I thought I could be special because of all of those old ladies who used to grab my face and pinch my cheeks and say things like, "Isn't she just adorable?" and "Isn't she precious?" At the time, it never occurred to me that maybe these were just the kind of things old ladies said about you when you were three or four and your mom carted you around because she didn't have any friends she could ask to babysit. I believed the hype.

After sitting alone for a miserable hour and a half, I caved in and called Conchita. She agreed to meet me for lunch, and as soon as she arrived, she immediately launched into another one of her fascinating stories about her work-related triumphs and achievements.

I sat there, listening, trying not to cry over what a disappointment I'd turned out to be, wishing that Conchita could be the kind of person that could make lonely people feel not so alone, but something told me there was a greater chance of me changing myself than of me changing her. So, I tried to listen and be supportive and hold back my tears until I could be alone.

After she left, I tried to remember the exact moment Conchita switched from envying me to pitying me. I remember when we were kids, she always used to say, "You're so lucky" about everything, like when I made the cheerleading squad and she didn't, even though it had been her idea to try out. "You're so lucky," she said when Dirk asked me out, as if I didn't deserve him. I didn't think I did, at the time, especially when I saw the way all the girls looked at me when we walked down the hall together, like I'd won the lottery and they hadn't. And Dirk had eaten it up, drinking in all of their envious stares, and as the years went on, soliciting them from women everywhere we went, constantly looking for opportunities to prove that he was still sought after.

I never looked around to see how many guys were constantly eyeballing me, making Dirk feel lucky to be with me, which, I suppose is why he left. He stopped feeling lucky.

I guess Conchita stopped thinking that I was lucky after she kissed Dirk that night I'd been too sick to go to Brian's party.

"You two go ahead," I'd said, stupidly thinking she would feel sorry and stay with me, foolishly hoping Dirk would say, "Well, I, for one, am not going without you, dear. After all, how could I have fun when my honey lamb is home sick?" For some reason people refuse to learn the lines you've scripted for them in your head, forcing you at all times to improvise.

She'd told me about the kiss the same night she told me she'd seen Dirk with another woman—the woman he'd run off with. We were drinking tequila shots—she said they would cheer me up, or make me forget—and she never could hold her liquor, so the story came out. She tried to deny it when I asked her about it later, but we both knew there was no point.

I made up my mind to tell her about the job offer as soon as she got home that night.

"Fantastic," she said. "Two successful career women. Tonight, we're going to celebrate."

We went to Cabana, the latest Latin hot spot, and lately Conchita's favorite place to hang out. It was loud and neon, pulsing and pixilated. As usual, Conchita headed straight to the dance floor. This was her turf. I didn't even try to join her.

A waiter approached me. "Do you want a table?" I think he asked.

It was hard to hear him over the music. "What? A table?"

"Let me get you a table."

I followed him to the back of the restaurant, and sat down at the booth he showed me.

"I'll send your friend back when she's finished," he said, smiling.

"Thanks."

After a while Conchita appeared, breathless. "Did you see the guy who asked me to dance? He's hot. And he's so intense. He was like, 'who are you?' 'where are you from?' You should go meet him."

"If he's so interested in you, what's the point?"

She shrugged. "He's from the same place in Cuba my grandmother is from. He knows all of my cousins. We're going to a club after dinner." This would have sounded a whole lot more impressive if it was not for the fact that Conchita was constantly meeting people from her family's hometown. Someone was lying, or it was a fairly large hometown.

I saw the waiter returning. "Are you ready to order?" I asked Conchita.

"You didn't order already? I always get the same thing here. Go ahead and order, I'm going to the little girls' room."

I ordered, and the food arrived as Conchita returned.

"Sorry," she said, "I ran into that guy again. He wants to go now. So, I was thinking, you can take the car. I'll get him to bring me home." And she was off again, leaving me alone with two dinners.

"Is everything okay?" the waiter asked. "Let me guess, you don't like the plantain. More like potatoes than bananas."

"No, that's not it."

"Well that's what I thought the first time I tried them. But I'm from the Mid-west. We don't get a lot of tropical food back home."

"I'd like a doggie bag."

He was the same waiter we had every time we'd come. He was extremely cute, and Conchita liked to flirt with him. He never fell for it, and paid equal attention to both of us.

"Your friend's not coming back, is she?"

"It's not the first time I've been stood up."

He looked at me quizzically for a moment. "Let me box up your food for you. I'll be right back."

He returned with two boxes. "Can I get you a drink? Come on, it's on me," he added when he saw me hesitate.

"I'll have a mojito."

"Great. I get off in five minutes. If you wait, I'll have one with you."

"It's been a long day. I'm really not in the mood."

"I know," he said. "But I'd like to talk."

So I waited. I had nothing better to do. It turned out his name was Mike and he was working his way through business school.

"What do you do?" he asked.

"I'm an actress. Sort of."

"Sort of?"

I told him all about my life, how I lived with my best friend from high school, and I'd been going on auditions for three years and I hadn't really had my break yet, unless you count an offer to be an assistant to a crazy has-been casting director.

"Maybe that is your big break. I mean, maybe it's not acting, but it is show business, and you'd be able to have your own life and stop sponging off your friends."

"I don't sponge of my friends."

"A futon? An '85 Honda? You want more than that, don't you? I can see it in your eyes."

"So, you think I should take the job?"

"I would. Not that what I say means anything. We barely know each other."

I looked at him over my mojito. "True. So why should I listen to a complete stranger?"

"We're not complete strangers. We're on a first name basis. And we've already made it through a cocktail. And besides, I know practically everything about you already."

I looked at him. His eyes were smiling, and I could see that it was true.

"So, Mike, tell me, when do you give up on a dream?"

"Maybe you don't," he said. "Maybe you alter it, to fit your current needs."

I finished my drink. "That's good, Mike. I like that. Because dreams are shapeless, temporal, easily maneuvered things, aren't they?"

"That's exactly what I mean. Another drink?"

"No. One drink a night with a 'not complete stranger.' That's my limit."

"I wish you'd stop referring to me as a stranger. We've known each other off and on, at least, four months. And now that we've had a drink, we should be good friends, don't you think?"

"Well, friends don't usually meet every now and then by chance. They often arrange meetings, dates, if you will."

Mike smiled and took a pen from his shirt pocket. "Yes, and in order to arrange these dates, they often exchange phone numbers."

He walked me to my car. "I'll call you tomorrow. I'm thinking maybe we could have dinner or something. You know, I'm glad we're friends."

As I drove home, I made up my mind to call Clara first thing in the morning to tell her I accepted her offer. I started to get excited at the thought of having to get up every morning with some place to go, of being responsible to somebody besides myself, saving money, getting a car, and finally moving out. It was as if a door was opening, and I had no idea where it would lead.

I started thinking about doing all of the things I never knew I wanted to do, and wherever I'd picture myself, Mike kept popping up inexplicably: in my car, sitting beside me on my new couch, lounging under an umbrella at the beach, playing tennis with me at the park.

I thought about how nice it would feel, sometime, to have a place of my own and to be alone, by choice. And that it might be nice to have dinner with someone I didn't have to prove myself to, someone who accepted me, someone who chose me.

Conchita was right, after all. There *were* too many people.

ELEVATOR MUSIC

She had been a flight attendant for exactly one week before being fired for spilling coffee and tomato juice on the same unfortunate, not to mention, sleeping passenger. Still, that annoying 'ding' that preceded even the most mundane communication was engraved on her consciousness as permanently as Theodore Roosevelt's face was etched on Mount Rushmore. Time and weather would eventually wear it down, but for now, it remained untouched, so much so that she half-expected to hear it every time her supervisor, Melody, spoke.

Ding.

"Those reports are due Monday."

Ding.

"Were there any messages?"

Ding.

"I want those copies done by the end of the day."

Ding.

"Tell the sales team the meeting starts in five minutes."

She'd been working the same temp job in the same high-rise building for almost two years. She was hardly temporary anymore, but she'd grown too lazy to look into becoming a permanent employee now. There would be so much paperwork to complete, and permanent had such an unpleasantly final ring, like a misspelled word written in ink that wouldn't be erased no matter how hard you rubbed.

Thousands of people probably passed through the lobby of the building on any given day. Nevertheless, in the two years she'd been there, she probably hadn't seen more than a handful of the people who worked there with her. Even more amazing, confined in the same building as they were, she rarely saw the same person twice. When she did see someone, she would try to figure them out, to place them in their natural habitat. She liked to think she had become a good reader of people. "He plays video games with his geeky friends after work," she would say about the thirty-something man wearing baggy cargos and a tee shirt beneath an unbuttoned flannel shirt. "She watches the Food Network and cooks gourmet dinners for her boyfriend who's really in love with his co-worker," she'd guess about the young professional woman in cashmere carrying a designer bag, fiddling with her Smartphone.

They would appear, like the dew, and briefly deliver their performances before vanishing forever behind closing elevator doors.

Ding.

She wondered if Burt, the guy behind the desk in the lobby, knew who they all were and where they all belonged. Most of them, she imagined, never spoke to him, choosing instead to rush past him on their way up, the way you would ignore a ficus tree or a cheap imitation of an ancient nude Roman.

Only the elevator slowed them down.

Ding.

Once inside, they'd look around. If they happened to know someone, they'd speak. Otherwise they kept their silence.

They'd stare at the stainless steel elevator doors or at the ceiling, anything to avoid eye contact, anything to avoid giving the impression that they thought they inhabited the same planet. Only if someone would sneeze would some brave soul, usually somewhere deep in the back of the elevator, dare to offer a mumbled, almost apologetic "bless you." Then they'd return to their prescribed silence. Los Angeles with its millions of people constantly traveling its congested freeways seemed small and user friendly compared to this building.

Traveling home from work, occasionally she'd get stopped at a certain light somewhere along Hyperion, and if it was the right time of day, just as night was settling in, and the lights were on in the coffeehouse on the corner, it would be like watching a Currier and Ives postcard of early rural America. The warm glow of the orange lights would bathe the furniture in such an inviting glow, she'd feel something inside like the gentle nudge of someone trying to remind her to do that thing she could never quite remember not to forget. Or she'd see a young couple about her age sitting at an intimate table, and by the intense way they spoke to one another she could tell that they were in love, and suddenly she would feel that they were all part of one of those quaint, old-fashioned movies set in some nameless small town about simple, honest people who grew up together and got married and raised children in the house one of them had grown up in, back when milk was delivered to the kitchen door in glass bottles, long before people had heard of serial killers and single-parent families and landfills overrun with plastic.

She'd forget that Los Angeles was large and anonymous, and for a moment she'd feel happy knowing she was not alone, but part of that elusive, collective notion celebrities and politicians were always referring to when they spoke of 'giving back to the community.' She'd be overcome by a feeling of intimacy and immediacy, so much so, that she'd have to lower her eyes like a self-conscious school girl talking to her first crush.

Other times, if the light wasn't right, she'd randomly catch someone's eye as he waited for his drink, and it would occur to her that this was someone she would never see again. He would disappear forever into that sea of faces that seemed to ebb and flow with its own predictable rhythmic timing, the way traffic seemed to have its own peculiar logic, enigmatically slowing, then just as erratically starting up again as if it had been steadily moving all along, in such a way that you could never plan for but found yourself a hapless victim in its unsympathetic clutches. Then she could stare brazenly; who would notice anyway?

Ding.

Whenever she entered an enclosed space, the first thing she did was look for an escape route. Experience had taught her this was usually best.

The lights above looked like a good bet with their removable plastic panels. She could probably manage to hoist herself up and raise one of them just enough to reveal the crawl space above, the cables, all the things that made the elevator work. She could get out. That was the important thing.

Airplanes always had a very clear escape route mapped out. Turn this. Pull that. In case of emergency, your seat may be used as a floatation device. In a way it was comforting. You always knew exactly what to do.

What she liked about the building were the badges all of the employees wore. They were laminated and had a photo, a sticker, and an expiration date. She wore hers around her neck with a black cord, just like the ones worn by all the other employees from the other buildings. She knew they were from different buildings because when she saw them walking on the street at lunchtime she noticed that their badges were different from hers. Different shapes, different colors, different orientations, the photos were in different locations. They belonged someplace else.

The badge answered those persistent questions: who am I, where am I going, why am I here? Not the way Gauguin meant, of course, but in a very concrete, global positioning kind of way that she found reassuring.

"Do you know what today is?" Bill, the salesman who sat next to her was leaning towards her, whispering.

He seemed to think that their proximity entitled him to conversation. She resented the way his too-pale skin sagged around his knuckles as if he was wilting from not enough sunlight, or the way his hands slightly shook when he tried to hand her a piece of paper, as if she made him nervous.

"The eleventh," she said. It was a morning ritual with him. He never knew the date, even though all he had to do was look at the bottom of his computer screen to find it.

"September eleventh," he said. "Five years later."

"Yes," she said, and then she was quiet. She thought the polite thing would be to ask if he thought it meant anything but realized it would only prolong the conversation. She thought him exactly the type who thought it sounded interesting to say things like, "I value long walks on the beach, poetry readings, and foreign films," in his online personal ad. She didn't know for a fact that he had an online personal ad, but he seemed to her to be exactly the type.

At lunch, they rode down in the elevator together.

"Can I buy you a cup of coffee?" he asked when they got out. He seemed to be thinking. She imagined he was trying to think of exactly the right line from a poem or something witty he'd heard in a movie.

"No thanks," she said. She looked at the exit across the

lobby. Burt was holding the door for a delivery guy delivering somebody's new desk. "Hold the door for me," she wanted to yell. She felt the walls closing in on her. Her escape plan was starting to look a bit fuzzy in the back of her mind, like a sidewalk chalk drawing someone had turned the garden hose on.

"I know you drink coffee," Bill said. "It'll just take a minute. My treat. Please."

The door closed behind the delivery guy, and she had the sensation that the air was being sucked out of the building.

The next thing she knew, she was sitting opposite Bill in the corner coffeehouse, waiting for her coffee to cool down.

"I used to worry about the end of the world ever since we went to the Griffith Park observatory in fifth grade," she found herself saying.

"I've never been there, myself. I've lived in LA for fifteen years, and there's so much I haven't seen. You know, *Rebel Without a Cause* was filmed there."

"I never saw it," she said.

"It was the defining movie of my generation. James Dean and Dennis Hopper. Those guys were so cool."

"Who's Dennis Hopper?" She'd heard of James Dean. There was that famous painting of him sitting at a lunch counter with some other dead celebrities. Once, she'd seen it in a video store at the mall, and her mother pointed them out to her. "Marilyn Monroe, Humphrey Bogart, James Dean," she had said. She remembered studying the scene. They all looked so young and happy, as if frozen in a perfect moment of time.

"I can't believe you don't know Dennis Hopper," Bill said. "He was huge back in the day. Now he does commercials for a retirement plan, which just goes to show how old we're getting."

She tried to imagine Bill young, but the skin on his hands looked especially fragile as he gripped his coffee cup, and she simply couldn't picture it.

"So what exactly about this field trip to Griffith Park made you conclude the world was ending?" He had apparently given up on finding something witty to say.

"They told us that the universe was expanding, that someday the sun would envelope everything and we would all burn up. It seemed believable, at the time, because it was based on astronomy and science. It's sort of like that Al Gore documentary. I guess you could say I'm a sucker for calamity howlers."

"No. You're cautious. And I suppose when you hear things like that when you're young, it makes a big impression."

"It's just that ever since then I've felt a huge cloud hanging over our heads. Things like Nine-Eleven just make it seem even more real."

Bill nodded. "I never thought I'd see anything like that. I grew up during the Cold War, so as kids, we expected the Communists to blow us up on a daily basis. But they're gone now. I suppose we got soft."

"I don't know what any of it means," she said. She swirled her coffee around in her cup. She hoped no one passing the coffeehouse would look in and assume they were in love.

"Time to get back?" Bill asked.

She looked at the clock on her cell phone. An hour was gone. She collected her empty sugar wrappers and napkins, and they went back to the office.

At lunch the next day, she found herself sharing the elevator with Bill again. The two of them stared ahead, as the elevator began its descent.

Ding.

The door opened halfway down, and two people—a man and two women—got in.

"You should get Amber to help you," one of the women said. "She loves to help people move."

Amber glared at her.

"Oh, yeah?" the man asked absently. "How 'bout it, Am? You, me and a dolly."

"I'm actually busy this weekend," Amber said.

"I don't blame you. Next time, I'm hiring movers," he said and the two women laughed.

The elevator opened and the three of them walked off.

"Would you like to get coffee?" she asked Bill as they stepped out the elevator. "I guess I owe you one."

Bill looked as if he was considering the idea. "Okay," he finally said. Definitely long walks on the beach, poetry readings, foreign films and wine tasting, she thought. He was such a cliché.

"My kids are ten and twelve," he said, emptying the contents of three packs of sugar substitute into his coffee, "a boy and a girl."

"I remember ten and twelve," she said, "almost as if it was yesterday."

"It was," he said. "You're still an infant."

"I'll be thirty in two years," she said. "The Challenger explosion was my defining moment. Up until that point, I really believed anything was possible. Then it all came crashing down."

"For me, it was the moon landing. It taught us that we could do anything. The sky was the limit, literally."

"And now they're saying it never happened," she couldn't help but laugh. She didn't want him to think she was laughing at him, but still, it was ironic.

"But I was there," he said. "I saw it on TV. Why do they try to steal our memories?"

"I don't know. But it's on the Internet."

"That's another thing, we didn't have the Internet when I was a kid. And I can't help but think it was better back then. If we needed information, we went to the library and made photocopies. We were patient. We didn't just Google stuff, and then cut and paste it into our reports. We typed and used carbon paper. If we made a mistake we started over or tried to rub it out with an eraser. Do kids today even know what microfiche is?"

She looked at him. He seemed so calm and quiet that she wondered if he had questions and doubts. She wondered if he really liked long walks on the beach.

"You know what's worse?" she asked. "Kids today get Nine-Eleven for their defining moment. It'll be the thing that changed who they are and what they believe in."

"I was talking to my son right after Nine-Eleven. I said, 'Imagine if you'd been in one of those buildings when the plane hit.' I was thinking aloud, I suppose. I hadn't really thought about how it had affected him. But he just sort of laughed and said, 'Big deal. You would've been dead.' That's when it hit me. Kids today are so desensitized. Maybe it's the movies or the video games. It's almost like they're a different breed."

"Or maybe he had to tell himself it was 'no big deal.' Otherwise the world's just a big, scary place that he doesn't fit into."

Bill looked at her, as if he was seeing her for the first time. "Maybe," he said.

"I think the saddest part of it is that all of those people died at work, in a building full of people they didn't know, probably doing stupid tasks they didn't want to do. They probably hated their jobs, hated their co-workers and their bosses. They probably only went to work that day because they had bills to pay. It doesn't seem fair."

"You just feel that way because you don't particularly like your job. But it's just a temporary assignment. You'll find your niche. We all do."

She was sure he wanted to believe that, but she'd seen how he looked after the weekly sales meetings with Melody.

"I just don't want to die doing something I hate," she said. She thought he looked uncomfortable, and she was sorry she'd said it, but they were being honest, and it seemed like the right thing to say.

"It's about time to get back," he said.

She was composing a memo to email out to the sales team about the punctual submission of expense reports when Melody breezed into the office.

Ding.

"Oh good, you're back. And you, too, Bill. Just so you know, I'm leaving early today, but tell Mark I'll be in at eight o'clock tomorrow." And she was off.

Bill chuckled softly. "She's just like a robot, that one," he said. "No hi or goodbye, just a carefully worded speech and an exit."

She laughed. "By the way, which one's Mark?"

"Exactly." Bill gathered his things. He hesitated. "Did you want to grab a bite to eat?"

"No," she said.

She typed a few lines on her computer and clicked send. First thing tomorrow morning the temporary agency would get her letter of resignation and there would be a new temp for Bill to talk to.

She collected her possessions from her desk drawers and put them in a plastic bag she found stuffed in a drawer in the break room. As she closed the office door behind her, she noticed that the hallway ahead seemed unusually wide and well-lit. She silently ticked off the seconds as she waited for the elevator.

"Twenty, twenty-one, twenty-two..."

Ding.

The elevator door opened. A middle-aged man wearing a security hat was staring at the ceiling. She smiled at him as she entered the elevator. "Hello," she said, "did you have a nice day?"

For a moment he said nothing. Then as the elevator door began to close, he answered: "Yeah, but it sure feels good to go home. My daughter-in-law just had a baby. Our first grandchild. How was your day?"

"Honestly, I've had better."

"Well, like they say, tomorrow's another day."

"That is what they say, isn't it?"

His cell phone rang and he looked around the elevator, as if he wasn't certain whose phone it was, although there were only two of them. He fished it out of his pocket and answered it. "I'm in the elevator," he said, "and the reception's bad. Let me call you right back." He closed his phone and put it back in his pocket. "My son," he told her.

"Well, congratulations on the baby," she said. "Boy or girl?"

"A boy."

Ding.

The door opened, and he followed as she exited the elevator.

"Thanks for asking," he said. "Nice riding with you. See you around."

She watched as he headed for the garage. "See you around," she called after him, knowing how unlikely that would be.

She waved to Burt as she passed him. "Good-bye," she called. She noticed for the first time, the soothing finality of that word.

PEANUT BUTTER SOUP

Peanut butter soup is how she will describe it years later, but for now, she swallows dutifully, although she could hardly describe herself as dutiful. Her sister had been the dutiful one, and look how that had turned out.

The first time she tasted his mother's culinary offering she'd known intuitively—the way she always knew things—that it would never work. Each handful of the warm, oily meat with mushy rice made it plainer. As she forced down each handful, she tried, with equal alacrity, to suppress the realization that she could not eat this for the rest of her life.

They'd met two years ago at a bookstore. Generally, when people asked how they met, she'd smile evasively and say she didn't remember.

The truth was, she was embarrassed to reveal how she'd been looking for a book on Southeast Asian cooking when he reached over her for a book on Sudanese food, how she'd glanced up at him and smiled absently, just to be polite, and their eyes had locked in a frighteningly real moment that was broken only when he muttered the almost inaudible words: "God, you're gorgeous."

Instinctively she closed her book and tried to leave the aisle. "I'm sorry, I've startled you," he continued. He sounded so formal, so unlike his initial outburst which, of course, he later denied saying.

"But, I heard you," she would say in her teasing tone.

"But, I don't talk like that."

"Maybe you do when you see a pretty girl," her eyes crinkling at the corners and her voice playfully challenging, points completely wasted on him.

He would admit, however, that when he first saw her, he had been stunned by her beauty, and no one had ever said anything like that to her before.

They would marry; she felt certain of it, because he believed in marriage and family, and recently he'd started saying that they should get married.

"Why?" she asked, one night over dinner when he first broached the subject. They had tried a new wine with dinner and she was feeling punchy.

"I'm twenty-eight," he answered. "My parents think it's time."

His frank answer nearly took the breath out of her. She had always imagined that one day her future husband would explain the reason for his proposal, with a breathless recounting of her qualities and idiosyncrasies. "Because I love the way you subscribe to *Time* just for the movie reviews," he would say. Or, "I love how you'd drive twenty miles for that perfect cup of coffee," ultimately ending with the declaration: "And when weighing everything, I realized that I could no longer breathe without you."

The truth was her habits annoyed him. He imagined, in time, he would break her of them, after explaining to her how illogical they were. She was, after all a reasonable woman, if 'reasonable' could be used to describe women.

Still, when all was said and done and accounted for, she did, at least, find some satisfaction in knowing that if the time had come for him to marry, he had chosen her. He was, after all, unlike the other men she had dated. Honorable. Decent. Polite. And somehow, knowing that he considered her a worthy partner made her feel honored. Although 'honored' didn't quite describe how she felt. But, she was twenty-eight, too, and she didn't want to be alone forever.

"Well, why not?" she would find herself thinking, whenever she allowed herself to consider his proposal. Though far from the emotionally charged feeling she had always gotten from watching Disney movies, she had to admit that she was not a European fairy princess riding off in a gilded carriage to live happily ever after, was she? She was a real person, and this was real life. And real life tasted like a handful of smoked turkey simmered in peanut butter sauce. Peanut butter was tolerable in small doses, but it was thick and heavy, and had the tendency to stick in one's throat.

She put her hand to her mouth and ran to the bathroom.

"Come back, daughter, I have not finished my story," his father called after her.

"She'll be back, Father," Jeff told him. "Don't worry."

She began to avoid him, mentally and emotionally at first. He would talk of their future together, and she would glance out of the window of his car, focusing on the people milling about the street or waiting at the bus stop. She would single out one person in the crowd, whoever happened to catch her eye, and she would study him or her intently. "Is he happy?" she would wonder. "Is she content?" Surely there would be some outward sign of happiness, some tell that she would recognize. If she could identify it, perhaps she could imitate it.

She stopped answering her phone, letting her voice mail pick up her calls. She would answer only if it was her mother, who worried when she didn't hear from her daily, or if it was one of those self-absorbed friends who could be depended on to launch right into their latest crisis without asking any personal questions.

"How's Jeff?" her mother would ask.

"He's fine," she would return, without giving it a thought.

That was the one thing she could set her watch by. He would always be fine. Not stressed out, not sad, not tired. He was dependable—she'd always liked that about him, except when it got on her nerves.

She used to think foreigners were so charming, so interesting, so sophisticated. If she and her sister happened to catch a hint of an accent when they were standing in line at and amusement park or while strolling through a museum, they would always turn and ask, "Where are you from?"

"How interesting," they would say, when the person said, "Italy," or "Australia," or "France." She and her sister would smile knowingly at each other, swept away in thoughts of sidewalk cafes, sleepy fishing villages, charming villas, anything different from home.

One day, she told her elderly Greek neighbor that she liked different cultures. She was taking her garbage out, and he was just returning.

"Why?" he asked.

She looked confused, so he added, "Culture is a big word. Be sure it means what you intend it to mean."

"What do you mean?"

"It involves learned behavior, feelings, thoughts, ways of viewing the world. It's not easily translated and doesn't always portray itself accurately to outsiders. That's why I say culture is a big word. You might like their food, but it doesn't mean you'll understand them."

"Hum," she said, trying to be tactful. "Perhaps that's been your experience..."

"I fought in the war," he interrupted, leaning against the trash bin and pointing emphatically to make his point. "I traveled the world—Europe, the South Pacific, Africa—I've been just about everywhere, and you know what I found out about foreigners? They come from different countries. That's it. They're not interesting. They're not special. They're the same as you and me. They just speak English with an accent. And you know what? They all think their way is the only right way. Imagine, an entire world of people who think they're the only ones with any sense!" He laughed.

She was watering the plants on her balcony the next morning before work, when she suddenly wondered why she'd gotten so annoyed the night before when Jeff called soccer football.

"Football's the thing that comes on Monday night, when the guys put on lots of padding and pat themselves on the behind." She tried to make a joke out of it. She said "behind" instead of "butt." But still, he pursed his lips like a prim schoolmarm.

"And they're miles, not kilometers," she added. "We learned the metric system in second grade, but it didn't catch on here."

"Well, the rest of the world caught on. You Americans are the only ones still using the British system. Even the British abandoned it ages ago."

"Well, when in Rome," she said. He smiled politely, but she knew that she had crossed some invisible line that only he could see, that she had turned into a rude American, an arrogant Ugly American. So she dropped the subject. Inside, however, she would stew.

Once she suggested that they go to the beach.

"What a wonderful night," she said, lingering outside his car. Dinner had been perfect, and only the beautiful full moon was lovelier than the warm breeze that beckoned them into the night. Besides, people in movies always went for walks on the beach.

She threw her head back, taking a deep breath. He stood apart from her, staring at her curiously, as if her exuberance frightened him.

"I know," she said conspiratorially, "let's go to the beach."

"It's late," he objected. Her eyes looked dark and wild. Uncivil, he thought, remembering she claimed to have Native American ancestors fairly high up on the family tree.

"It's ten o'clock. Come on, Jeff."

Reluctantly he got in the car and drove to the beach. He parked the car, reluctantly turning off the engine, as he stared straight ahead in stony silence.

She laughed. "Okay, technically, we are at the beach. But I was hoping we'd get out of the car," she said, opening her door.

He followed as she ran down to the beach. The sand felt warm between her toes. She laughed again, and reached for his hand. Looking down, she noticed he was still wearing his shoes.

"Well, you're supposed to take your shoes off, Jeff. Then, you roll your pants up, so you can feel the sand and the water. That's the whole idea."

Methodically, he began to remove his shoes and socks. Then, painstakingly, he started to roll up his pants, as if going to the beach was an annoying chore, rather than a spontaneous and romantic adventure. "Hurry up," she wanted to say. "This is supposed to be fun, not pulling teeth."

He began to walk, slowly and silently, and suddenly she wished she'd kept her suggestion to herself.

When he called her at work the next morning, he was his even-tempered self, causing her to wonder if his behavior the night before had been imagined.

His family began to indoctrinate her in their customs, and she was expected to forget or relegate any values she had been taught in favor of theirs, since Americans didn't have any customs, culture, or heritage to pass on. She resented this, because, on Fridays she and her sister rented movies and ordered Hot Lover's Chicken from Uncle Chen's, and if this wasn't a tradition, what was?

They began to spend more and more time with his family, and his parents would consistently turn down invitations from her parents.

Gradually she learned to decipher his thoughts and feelings. With this new understanding, she began to realize that everything they had done together had been a lie.

Once, he took her to see *Turandot*.

"Oh, look," she said, pointing to the calendar, "*La Boheme* is next. Let's go. It's the first opera I ever saw."

"I can't," he said, not looking at her. "I hate opera."

"Then why are we here?"

"It's the thing to do. But I can only do it every now and then. Definitely not two weeks in a row."

She looked at him, trying to process his words. How do you hate opera? How can you hate *Nessun Dorma*? How could two people see the same thing so differently?

The monumental importance of their discovered incompatibility did not hit him with the same force. So, they were not born compatible, they would learn the same manufactured compatibility his parents had. She would be molded and shaped as easily as she could be taught to cook peanut butter soup. And she would learn because she was a quick study, smart and diligent, unlike most Americans he'd known in school. They would be happy, because his parents were—it was a tradition.

His mother arrived at her apartment early Saturday morning. She could see her through the peephole, and for a split second, considered leaving her behind the locked door. Then it could be over that simply. His mother would go away; he would go away; and they would find some other girl to bear his children. She would go to the opera, and then for a walk on the beach.

"Don't worry," he would tell his father. "She's not coming back." But that wouldn't be polite.

So, she let her in, and they spent the whole day in the hot kitchen, cooking and learning, teaching and absorbing the methods and techniques, the smells and attitudes that would contribute to a perfect home and traditional family.

"He can cook," his mother told her. "But he will want his wife to learn."

As she stirred and chopped and mixed and tasted, she thought, "What about what I want?" She thought about long, moonlit walks on the beach with someone who would open his soul to her, but she wanted to be polite, so she didn't say anything.

When Jeff and his father arrived, she and his mother spread the traditional feast out before them. They ate the warm peanut butter stew, handful after handful, until every inch of her being was full and she was drowning in it.

Jeff's father was in the midst of describing the house he had found for them in that prominent neighborhood near the best schools, when she suddenly found herself pushing away from the table.

Jeff's father looked at her sharply. "What's the trouble, Daughter?"

Making her apologies politely, she was starting toward the bathroom when she—in one decisive move that shocked even her—turned toward the front door, and left without a word.

Calmly, deliberately, quite without passion, she got into her car and drove away.

When she returned several hours later, she found that Jeff and his parents had politely gone home. Funny thing, though, it was months before the smell of peanut butter was completely gone.

BLACK OUT

The trip to Italy had been glorious even though, at the last minute, business had made it impossible for Mike to come.

"Don't cancel on account of me," he'd said. "Maybe I can catch up with you two later." He hadn't, and Natalie and Dave had had fun without him.

Their days had consisted entirely of waking up early to beat the bands of loud and uninformed tour groups to points of interest, looking at magnificent art all day, and eating spectacular food at night. Mike didn't appreciate art and gourmet food the way Natalie and Dave did. He didn't revel in "culture," being more a self-proclaimed nuts and bolts, meat and potatoes kind of guy.

Dave made his confession inside one of the cathedrals. His mother asked him why he'd stopped going to church.

He tried to explain that it just wasn't relevant anymore. It was history. It was a grand building. It was a post card of a painting to stick casually on the refrigerator with a magnet. It didn't mean anything, not to him, not anymore.

"Don't you sense the great unknown?" Natalie asked. "Don't you ever wonder?"

"No," he said flatly, and wandered into the next room.

Natalie stared at the painting of the *Pietà*, vaguely wondering when precisely she had lost her son, and how exactly she had failed him. But a tour group from Poland was coming in to view the frescos, and Natalie needed to keep moving.

Dave had just graduated from law school, and Natalie and Mike couldn't be prouder. Dave had always been bright. My little man, she used to call him.

She would watch him pouring over his homework—subjects she couldn't even remember studying, like physics and geometry—and she'd wonder what magnificent things he would grow up to do.

The excitement and wonder gave her goose bumps at times, but she never told Mike. "Enjoy it now," he would have said. "Life's too short to worry about the future." He was a very here-and-now kind of guy, while Natalie lived in the realm of possibilities.

Like her, Dave was always yearning, always anticipating what was next, eager to be older, to be allowed to do the next thing on the rung of growing up.

At five, he'd insisted on standing at the curb, waiting to cross without holding her hand. When she accompanied his class on field trips, he pretended to be completely autonomous, barely acknowledging her existence. She went on all the field trips. She was always curious to know what he was learning.

Only now, in Italy, did she feel slightly self-conscious

to be the mother of a law school graduate. She didn't feel that old. She felt exactly the same way she felt when she first found out she was going to be a mother—scared, unequal to the challenge, but hopeful. She still felt that twinge of self-doubt, sometimes, not like Dave who always seemed so sure of himself.

The new generation was so confident, and that baffled her, since and the world was so much more complicated than it had been when she and Mike were young. They emailed and text-messaged one another, sharing their thoughts on the world, which was changing as fast as their ideas were transmitted. But they were determined to keep in constant communication via email, and IMs and DSL, and PDAs and other devices with initials she still had a hard time deciphering. She knew Dave thought her archaic because she was slow to embrace technology. She still felt a letter from a friend that arrived on a computer screen was cold and impersonal, preferring stationary with flowers, scrawling cursive, and hand-drawn smiley faces, instead of a colon and parenthesis.

"Very hot," the Nigerian cab driver said, as he reached for Dave's duffle bag.

"Yes," Natalie agreed. Europe had been unusually hot that summer, more like California at the height of burn season.

On the frantic ride to the airport, Natalie watched their trip replay through the cab window, like an amateur Power

Point presentation. "My Italian Holiday," the title would read. Pictures of cobblestone streets and cafes and statues would flash on and off the screen while Andrea Bocelli sang in the background.

They sped past an apartment building, and Natalie watched an elderly Italian woman beating a rug on her balcony. The dust flew off in slow billowing clouds that only reluctantly settled over the street. The old woman stopped for a moment, staring at the cab as it flew past, and Natalie recoiled at the thought of dying from heat stroke in a hot Roman apartment, like so many had already, according to all of the news reports.

At the airport, they breezed through one security checkpoint after the other. Crowds of summer tourists were being herded through the airport like cattle, and Natalie and Dave didn't have a chance to talk until they were settled on the plane.

"Mom, how'd you know Dad was the one?" Dave asked when all of their baggage had been neatly tucked away.

"I didn't," she answered. "But I'd already turned someone else down. I was young. I thought he'd ask again, but he didn't. And that's when I met your dad. He was a nice guy. But it was never like that with us."

"You settled," Dave said, looking past her at the woman in the next row who was struggling to console her small child.

"Well," Natalie said quietly, "I got you out of it."

She closed her eyes, but she couldn't sleep.

Perhaps she shouldn't have been so honest with Dave. He'd looked at her with such raw disappointment. But when she thought about the woman beating the rug on the balcony, she couldn't glamorize things.

She thought she felt Dave staring at her, so she opened her eyes. He was trying to read the in-flight magazine, but he kept staring at the same page. She touched his arm lightly, and he turned to her.

"You know, I asked about you and Dad because you've always seemed like the perfect couple, and I wanted some advice. I've been seeing someone."

"Oh," Natalie said, stupidly. "Oh, I see. Is it serious?"

"I think she's the one, Mom." Dave was smiling, as if he'd burst with happiness. "I love her. She makes me a better person."

"What's she like?"

"She's amazing."

"Amazing, how?"

"I don't know. She's not like you or me. She's a bit like Dad, to tell you the truth. But it works, you know."

Natalie nodded. "I do."

Dave nodded in return, still smiling.

In New York, while they waited for their flight home, Natalie and Dave stopped at a diner to have the kind of breakfast Natalie used to make when Dave was a kid, before everything had gotten so complicated. They talked about pets they'd had, driving lessons, family vacations, and first dances.

Dave reproached Natalie for punishing him for his rare and ridiculous boyhood capers, while Natalie teased Dave for his skater phase. Each time she laughed, she had the sensation that a tiny piece of her was escaping, so tiny it was scarcely noticeable, as if a massive, unseen constrictor had wrapped itself around her gut, tighter and tighter with each exhalation, until she was completely asphyxiated.

At the airport, Dave went to get coffee while they waited for their fight to be called. Natalie was thumbing through last week's issue of *Newsweek* when the power went off.

There was a slight popping sound, then everything seemed to grind to a halt. Suddenly there was dimness and an unfamiliar silence.

"What's going on?" the businessman sitting across from her asked absently but continued to scan the report he had been reading.

"Is it a bomb?" an elderly woman asked. "Is it terrorists?" She looked at Natalie, frightened.

Natalie smiled. "No," she said, and the woman went back to napping.

When Dave returned, he told Natalie that the airport had lost power, but they felt it would be up again momentarily.

People waiting nearby started to call friends and family.

"I don't think it's just the airport that's lost power," one girl said, "I think it's the entire city."

"Well, I'm not getting a signal on my cell phone," another passenger said, drawing an irrational conclusion.

"Did you want to try to call Dad?" Dave asked, offering Natalie his cell phone.

"I think I'll wait till I have more information. You know how your father is about details," she told him.

"Well, I'm going to go outside for bit," Dave said. "I'll be right back."

Natalie could see him from her seat inside. He walked around several minutes, trying to get a signal on his cell phone. Finally, he dialed and began talking to someone on the other end. He was smiling and laughing, and suddenly Natalie got the feeling she was watching someone she had never seen before.

"You were talking to her?" Natalie asked when he returned to his seat.

"Yes. I wanted her to know I was okay."

"I could tell. You were glowing." Natalie said, and so strong was the feeling that she had intruded on an intimate moment that she almost apologized.

Dave went away again, and when he returned he had two bottles of water.

"The airport's passing them out," he told her. "I have a feeling we're going to be here a while."

Natalie took a nap while Dave watched their bags.

Around five o'clock, Natalie went off to see if she could find sandwiches, but all of the vendors had run out around two o'clock.

She returned empty-handed, shrugging at Dave.

"But," she told him, "people are starting to line up."

They collected their things and went back to the ticket counter. The line trailed well outside. A group of twenty-somethings with backpacks and body-piercings were sitting on the floor ahead of them. Every time the line advanced, one of the girls would scoot forward on her rear end. So unladylike, Natalie thought, grateful the girl was not her daughter.

The check-in process was tedious without computers. By the time Natalie and Dave were ushered to the boarding gate, it was nearly two in the morning.

"We're trying to get a flight out to Los Angeles," the airport employee announced to the crowd. He was holding a clipboard and a flashlight. "Our generators should be up soon."

Natalie smiled reassuringly at Dave. They sat down near the window. Outside was pitch black, but there was a distant glow that seemed to announce the coming dawn.

Dave fell asleep immediately. Inch by inch his body relaxed and his breathing became heavy.

As Natalie watched him, she became increasingly aware of the sensation that this man was not the little boy whose clothes she'd washed and whose permission slips she'd signed. He didn't belong to her anymore.

Absently, she stroked his forehead, and he turned in his seat without waking.

After several minutes Natalie heard a familiar buzzing, and the lights flickered on. The sleep-starved crowd at the boarding gate broke into half-hearted applause.

"It'll just be another minute folks," the man with the clipboard said.

Finally, they were loaded onto the plane. Dave sighed.

"Before you go back to sleep, can I borrow your cell phone?" Natalie asked.

Dave fumbled for it and handed it to her.

Very carefully she dialed her home phone number. Mike answered after exactly two rings. "I heard about the blackout," he said.

"Yes," she answered. "I'll be a little late, but I wanted you to know, I'm coming home."

THIN ICE

The ice rink was a dingy-looking building near the outskirts of town. Bradley found it by accident one day on his lunch break. He'd been driving around the Valley, trying to find a store some girl at work had told him about—the one that sold those cool tee-shirts with the slogans that really amounted to giving someone the finger but looked like a big, silly smiley face.

Realizing he was going the wrong way down the wrong street, he pulled into the big empty parking lot, and saw the words "Valley Ice Rink" fading from the sign on the building. Suddenly he remembered the time when he was seven—the first time he'd ever stepped into a rink—when his mom had taken his brother and him to the local ice rink to ask about hockey lessons. The rink had been cool, which felt strange after riding around so long in the summer heat. He remembered the sound, a soothing, rhythmic swish of blades on the ice as his mom talked to the coach who'd met them in the lobby. The next thing he knew, he and his brother were signed up, swept into the fierce competitiveness and perpetual frenzy of forced friendships.

After the divorce, they didn't have money for things like hockey lessons, so he took up video games and his brother played softball, while his one-time teammates skated their way to intramural glory.

He told himself he was only there to turn around but found himself stopping the car, going inside, and asking about the public session.

"You can skate now, if you want," the teen-age girl behind the counter told him. She seemed a little flustered, but most girls acted flustered around him, he noticed. A girl at work explained to him it was because he had the fatal Brad Pit/ Johnny Depp combo: little boy with an edge. He didn't know where he had gotten it. He was just an accountant from Pacoima.

"It's kind of nice because no one's come in yet," she said, "except her. She comes every day."

He looked at the ice where the girl was pointing. A young woman was skating listlessly in circles on the ice. "She won't mind. She never notices anyone."

He rented a pair of skates and went down to the ice.

The woman looked up as she skated past the opening in the gate where he stood, until he could catch the momentum he needed to step on the ice, not changing her expression, which was steady and penetrating.

"I'm sorry," he called out. "I'm sorry to disturb your solitude." It sounded ridiculously formal, like he watched too much Masterpiece Classics on the weekend, but somehow she called for that. He hoped the girl out front wasn't listening—Johnny Depp would never have said something so stupid.

The woman slowed and glided to a stop. He noticed she had wonderfully perfect posture. "I don't mind," she said. Her voice was beautifully sad, melancholy, but musical. She had big, dark eyes, and a somber mouth. Her thick, dark hair was pulled delightfully into a ponytail, which was the only cheerful thing about her. She was dressed in jeans and a big, chunky sweater, which seemed to move independently of her when she skated. As she spun, the sweater hovered over the ice, making its own circles, independent of her movement which somehow seemed suspended, as if time had stopped with her posed perfectly above it.

He found himself stopping to watch her, like a kid watching a music box in fascination. Where does it come from? How does it work? How do I know that I'm not in a music box and someone's making me move? A ridiculous smile crept onto his face, and he couldn't make it go away.

The more she skated, the more he felt that someone was ripping him apart. Pathos was a word he remembered from high school, and it was finally dawning on him what it meant.

"You're amazing," he told her. They were sitting on benches, taking off their skates. School was out, and they both decided to quit before the kids invaded the rink.

"Thanks," she said.

"Are you a professional?"

"No."

"I guess that's the wrong word. Competitive, I mean. Are you a competitive skater?"

"No." She took her skates off, slipped on a pair of flip-flops, and stood to leave.

He had figured they'd walk out together, but she had already turned toward the door.

"See you around," he said.

She seemed to nod, he thought, but later, he wasn't sure. He knew she walked off, because he could still see that slow, determined swing.

She could do perfect spins, dozens of rotations, all in one spot. She'd spin and spin and when she'd stop, there'd be a small circular scratch on the ice. "That's what they look for," she'd say. "You're not supposed to travel." She could do it, she explained, because she had a low center of gravity.

She would try to teach him, demonstrating again and again, till he was certain she'd faint from dizziness. It was spotting, she'd say. Keep your eyes on something, a spot on the wall, maybe. Your head should be the last part of your body to leave that spot, the first to return. If you did it right, you wouldn't get dizzy.

So, he'd try, inevitably collapsing before her. Once, she'd caught him, and he feared all one hundred seventy-five pounds of him would come crashing down on her, but she bore it, steadying him, like a fragile tree in a storm.

He bought her a cup of hot chocolate one day when they decided to take a break, and she sat at the table with him while she drank it.

"What do you do, Bradley?" she asked. It was the first time she'd shown any interest in his life.

"I'm an accountant," he said.

"I'm a housewife," she said. "My husband's a successful businessman. He's never home. I used to think he worked so hard for me. But I realize now that he likes to collect things. He never uses them; he just looks at them every so often." She pulled the sleeves of her sweater over her hands. "I hate to be looked at. Sometimes," she looked at him with her penetrating eyes, "sometimes, I want to escape."

Bradley wanted to take her in his arms and hold her. She was so brave, so alone. He wanted her to know that he would be there for her.

"But, no matter what, I still believe in marriage. I have to believe in something."

They had met ten years ago in Japan. She was there for an ice skating competition. He was in town on business, staying at the same hotel. There seemed to be a mix-up with her luggage and he helped sort it out. He asked her to meet him for drinks, and she felt it was the least she could do. One thing led to another and before she knew it, they were engaged. She had been eighteen, barely a woman, and she'd never had a boyfriend before. Those four a.m. practice sessions didn't leave much time for a social life.

Her coaches had wanted her to train for the Olympics, but she was tired. Her parents wanted her to go to college. She didn't know what she wanted, and if she was married, no one would have a say.

"I was tired of the competition," she explained. "Tired of someone having to lose for someone else to win. I wanted to win, until I realized I was hoping some other girl would fail. I used to wonder why we couldn't all get what we wanted. Success shouldn't come at someone else's expense."

"I bet you were good," he said, his eyes full of admiration.

She smiled quietly. "I had my moments."

She was so pure and so good that he felt dirty for wanting her, wishing her husband would lose, so he could win.

They went back to the ice. As they skated together, he felt closer to her than he'd ever felt to anyone before.

As soon as he got home, he searched the Internet for videos of her competitions. He watched, mesmerized. While he had been frittering his adolescence away on the futile pursuits of playing video games and applying Clearasil, she had been busy making magic. He understood why she gravitated to the ice rink.

He kicked himself for being too late, for meeting her, for thinking about her, for wanting her.

Eventually, he stopped going to the rink, telling himself he was too busy. Then one day, he got a call at work. She was on the line, asking him to meet her at Starbucks.

"It's been a long time," she said, smiling, as he sat down. She looked happy to see him, but uneasy. She kept looking at the cell phone on the table in front of her. "My husband usually calls around this time," she explained.

Bradley looked at the phone in disgust. She was like a

caged bird, he thought.

"I missed you," he told her. "But I had a lot of work."

"I thought you liked to skate. I go every day. I looked for you. It wasn't the same without you."

"I would have come, if I thought you really wanted me to."

"I did."

Bradley looked at her, looking for a sign. He reached across the table and took her hand, but she pulled it away. Her head was down, and he thought she was crying.

"I shouldn't have asked you to come," she said after a while.

"Why?"

"Because you're in love with me," she said in her calm, matter-of-fact way.

He felt keenly that there was no point in denying it. He wanted to ask her if she loved him. "Then, why did you?" he said at last.

"I don't know," she answered.

"I stopped coming because I wanted to forget about you," he finally said.

"You should," she said. "You'll find someone else. And I'll be fine."

"But will you be happy?" he asked.

"I don't want to be happy. Not like this. I won't quit, Bradley. I want to see it through."

"Is that enough?" he asked. "Is it?"

"It's what's right," she said.

"I'll never find anyone like you," Bradley finally said. "There isn't anyone."

The phone rang. She looked frightened but reached for it as if by reflex.

"Is it him?" he asked.

"Please," she said, "leave me alone."

She answered the phone and Bradley walked to the door.

"I'm fine," he heard her saying. "I'm just getting coffee."

Bradley never went back to that skating rink, but sometimes, when he passed an old dilapidated building, he remembered how close he'd come to destroying something beautiful.

INTENDED PURPOSE

Her hands moved across the keypad as if they had a mind of their own. If not their own mind, certainly their own rhythm. She was sending a text.

Her fingers moved like nuanced dancers, the result of muscle memory. Automatic. Routine.

These days, they rarely communicated if not by text, not since the wedding, anyway. Before the wedding, before the *engagement*, they had been in love, deeply and profoundly in love. Their conversations would go late into the night, filled with all of the good things they needed to hear, liberally peppered with terms of endearment. Words like honey, babe, darling, and dearest would spill out over into their conversations and she would fall asleep with him on her thoughts.

Now, they constantly texted each other. She was accustomed to looking at her vibrating phone and shooting off a message with little or no forethought. Her co-workers would exchange knowing looks. They knew she was a newly-wed and figured she and her husband couldn't get enough of each other. The truth was, their texts were strictly essential communications, often terse commands and reminders:

I don't think I locked the back door
I'll check.
No...it was locked

Don't forget to let the cat out

Don't forget to let the cat in

Is the iron off??!!!

Did you pu the dry cleaning?

WE NEED MILK

They hardly saw each other anymore. She couldn't remember if it was out of necessity or by design, but there it was. She left for work early. He did not.

For half the year, it was still dark out when she left and dark again when she returned home. On those mornings, it never ceased to surprise her how many people were already out and about making their way west on those network-like roads that supplied life to the city.

BART would be crowded. There was hardly a place to sit. Most riders were commuters, like her, but sometimes she would see elderly couples squeezing in with their luggage.

She imagined they were visiting their children, busy professionals who couldn't be bothered with such mundane things as airport drop-offs and pickups. Pity they hadn't timed their trip better.

Or sometimes there would be younger travelers who, but for their overly casual attire and their overabundance of baggage, might be mistaken for commuters. They crowded in, taking up more than their fair share of space with their luggage, made from that modern rip-stop fabric that never seemed to hold its shape, but bulged with inadequacy, over-stuffed, she imagined, with rolled up tee shirts and torn jeans.

She rode alone in the mornings. Her co-worker usually took a different train. So she would sit quietly and stare out of the windows or into space. If someone saw her in these moments, they would imagine her to be an unhappy person. This was not true. She was deeply and profoundly happy because she had every reason to be.

On the trips home, she and her co-worker caught the train together and rode together and conversed incessantly. She could tell the other riders were somewhat annoyed by their conversation which was too loud, too hip, too young, and too enthusiastic as they described with gusto the new and exciting twists and turns their lives outside work were taking. They were both newly married and had both just purchased new condos in the same brand new development.

Her husband, however, was just starting graduate school. Her co-worker's husband was not.

"Of course," she admitted, "it'll be an expense now. But it's for our Future."

"True," her friend agreed. "You have to think about the Future."

The future that loomed ahead of her, like the rolling hills they traveled through to get to work.

"It's an investment," she said. He had taken out a loan which they would add to their already burgeoning student loans, which had seemed like a good idea at the time, but were starting to feel like a premature declaration of love indiscreetly tattooed on one's body. It seemed impossible to her that they would ever finish paying them, but that mattered little; they, like the Boomers, would never get old.

"Yes," her co-worker said, silent for a moment. Then she asked: "Did you decide to go with the walk-in closet?"

"No," she said. "We opted for the sitting room. We decided we'd rather have the usable space."

"Well, we're getting the walk-in closet," her co-worker replied, even though she hadn't asked. "My husband's thinking about the re-sell value."

They hadn't even moved in and they were already thinking about selling, already concerned about moving up, already obsessed with upgrading.

Yes, she could tell they got on the nerves of their fellow riders—people who got off at stations just outside the City and apparently lived in dingy, graying neighborhood with little or no trees and perpendicular streets instead of the meandering, gently sloping neighborhoods she was used to.

They wore work boots and uniforms and apparently toiled away at dead-end jobs with no future and nothing to look forward to. They didn't make investments; they paid bills.

Her phone buzzed—a text from her husband:

B home late 2nite...another mtg :-(

She got off BART and transferred to the train.

Sometimes she wished they were characters in a Hemingway story. They would say nothing, but it would be full of subtext that the two of them would understand. They would speak in short, clipped sentences that would be as full of and, at the same time, as devoid of meaning as you felt inclined to impute to them at any given moment. He and she would be clever, witty, and sophisticated, sitting in bars outside train stations with their hard-sided leather luggage...*suitcases* bearing—like badges of honor—stickers and labels of all the places they'd been.

There would be comfort in the economy of words. Nothing would ever need to be taken back. Words wouldn't hang in the empty silence above them like wasted lines on a page. It would be like a dance. Counted out. Planned. Measured. Of course, her name would be Jig, and he would be a nameless slob.

She would have liked to bum her way through Europe, but there hadn't been time, what with the wedding and the planning.

But all of this was nonsense. She took her eReader from her bag and started to read. At least, she tried to read, but her thoughts kept distracting her.

During the summer months, the hills appeared rolling and smooth and tawny-colored like the backs of lions. Like undulating sand dunes, they seemed to wave and ebb although she knew, in reality, they were static, not at all like whimsical, mood-uplifting thoughts that came visiting at the most unexpected moments, but more like nagging doubts that clung tightly and tried their level best to spiral you to pits of melancholy.

To the right, she could see jack rabbits, a random coyote, and cows, always cows. Slow moving, ever grazing, dependable, unimaginative cows, that were always there, like watchmen over the valley's trespassers. The hills, she liked to imagine, stretched on forever. She liked the idea that things could be boundless and limitless, that they could drift to the edge and gently float over in a continuous flow, like those chocolate fountains they sometimes have at weddings.

She had wanted one. She had no idea why. She was not one of those women who loved chocolate, but it had seemed like a good idea. Someone though, probably her step-father, had vetoed it, which was well within his rights. He'd been more than generous in paying for the wedding. Except, she'd really wanted that decadent chocolate fountain.

To the left, she could see discarded junk—abandoned vintage cars, bones of long-dead cows, old tires, an obsolete mattress strewn along the way as if the train, as it cut its swath through the mountains, was leaving debris in its wake.

Several weeks before the wedding, she and her fiancé had been dinning out when he casually mentioned that he had invited her father to the wedding.

"Why?" she asked.

He looked shocked. "He's your father," he answered. "He should be included. He's wondering what role he'll play, by the way."

"Funny," she said, "I've been wondering that, myself, since I was a kid."

He bit his lip, obviously not amused, although she thought it was quite funny. "He's your father," he repeated.

"A mere biological fact," she said. "More than likely, a mistake."

He looked severe. His parents were celebrating their thirtieth wedding anniversary this year and said things like, "We're more in love today than we were when we first got married."

"I'll have to think about it," she said.

"What's to think about? He's your father."

"That's true. Actually, you already said that," she said and let the words hang above the table as they finished their meal in silence.

Weddings, after all, were not forums for logic and harsh realities; they were all about those sappy, feel-good, sentimental father/daughter, mother/son moments.

"Are you excited about the wedding?" her co-worker had asked.

"Yes and no," she answered. When her friend looked shocked—no, surprised—she added, "It's just that I almost wish it was over, you know, and that our life was starting."

In a way, that was how she felt. They'd been in such a hurry to get engaged. They'd set the date so long ago, and for the longest time, it had seemed to be marching toward them with the aggressiveness of an advancing army, confident of victory. Sometimes she wondered if they'd done it to lock themselves into something they both knew neither would have the courage to back out of. They knew they'd get swept away, carried along on the momentum they'd created.

They should have waited. There was plenty of time; they were still both so young. They should have waited until they had each become the person they were supposed to become and then see if they still wanted this. But perhaps this thing, this feeling wouldn't have lasted beyond the morning, like a light summer rain that would not survive the sunrise.

"Who's walking you down the aisle?" her co-worker had asked.

"Yeah, so that's the tricky part. I want my step-dad, since you know, he raised me, and I think of him more as a father. But my real father, my *biological* father, wants to come and everyone thinks it will look...odd if he doesn't give me away. He wants to play his role, but I guess I'm kind of over it."

Her friend looked shocked again, so she added, "You know, the drama."

"Oh yes," her friend said. "Who needs drama?"

It was hot in the train, and they were standing. Her co-worker was fanning her face with her hand as people unapologetically pressed on them. It looked like she was having a hot flash, but she was much too young for that.

She wished she would stop.

"How are you not hot?" her friend asked.

Because I'm not fifty, she wanted to say, but she only shrugged.

"Anyway," her friend said, "You're both coming for dinner on Saturday, right?"

"We'll be there," she answered, "unless he has to work." He'd been working a lot lately.

She glanced at her friend.

There was something troubling about the way her coat fit, or didn't fit, and the boots were a particularly unfortunate addition to the outfit. She looked rumpled and frumpy, but then, she always did. She was frumpy. From the way she kept adjusting her clothes, it was obvious that she knew it too.

On the other hand, for some reason, her clothes always seemed to fit. They always looked as if they had just come straight from the tailor's. Her black wool coat was as perfect at the end of the day as it had been when she put it on that morning. No wrinkles, not lint, no pet hair. Perfect. Neat.

In truth, her clothes always fit more like a costume—they were too perfect, too neat, too exactly according to the role she was assuming: student, bride, young professional, wife. They never seemed lived-in but gave the impression that if she would leave, the clothes would be completely capable of carrying on her life for her, a fully competent proxy.

She wondered absently if her friend felt embarrassed to stand next to her; if she knew she suffered by comparison, but she seemed too busy fanning away to be conscious of anything.

She glanced down at her left hand. The ring is what embarrassed her. It was almost too much of a statement. *My husband, the grad student, is climbing the corporate ladder,* it said. *One day soon, I will be his trophy wife.*

"So," her co-worker asked, "was it terribly exciting?"

"Yes," she'd said enthusiastically, even though it had not been. She didn't know exactly why it had not been exciting. Perhaps her mother's pragmatic question, "Really? That much?" had started it. They were not emotional people. Her mother wasn't about to get all weepy and teary-eyed like the mothers-of-the-brides on those reality TV shows. She seemed to feel that the first wedding was no big deal. Having been through two of her own, maybe she was right. Or maybe it was the fact that there never was the one dress that jumped out at them.

"They all look good on you," her grandmother had commented incredulously. And it was infuriatingly true, as if she had been born to wear wedding dresses. A-line, mermaid, princess, cathedral, tea-length. They all looked equally perfect, making a decision impossible.

She resorted to eeny-meeny-minney-mo, pretending to be over the moon happy in love with the dress, the dress she tagged "it." She would Tweet about it and post it on Instagram. "I found THE dress," she would say. In reality, she had found "a dress."

The city was cold today, but it seemed to always be cold in the city. People who lived there claimed that it warmed up over the weekend. "I was wearing shorts and flip-flops," they would boast as they marched off to expensive lunches at trendy spots, but it never seemed to go above seventy degrees during the work week. She imagined that the cold was preserving them all, like lettuce, but perhaps in the end, it was hastening their demise, as in the case of a bunch of bananas placed in the refrigerator by mistake.

It was Friday, and her co-worker's party was the next day. She was returning home alone on the late train because her co-worker had stayed home. Sick, she'd said, but she was probably doing last minute preparations for the party.

The house was empty when she got home. She let the cat in (he'd texted earlier to say he'd let the cat out), and she sat in the sitting room, ostensibly to read, but she sat, staring into space. Soon it was too dark to read, and she was too lazy to turn on the lamp. She sat, thinking about dinner, but she was too tired to head to the kitchen.

Her phone buzzed.

"I got Chinese," he wrote, and she began to cry.

On Saturday, they headed to Costco to purchase their regular, weekly items, their survival supplies. Stopping at a sushi bar for lunch, they sat quietly and ate. Every now and then her husband returned a text or an email while she looked out of the window at the parking lot outside.

They headed home to dress for the party. She put on her young, married, suburban weekend outfit, and he wore jeans and a sports coat.

Armed with a bottle of wine, they drove exactly one block over to a condominium that was identical to theirs, for all intents and purposes, where they were greeted enthusiastically by a set of hosts who, for all intents and purposes, were identical to them.

Her co-worker exclaimed over her jacket, and they were ushered into the master bedroom to the walk-in closet where they could stow their belongings for the duration of the party.

She gave her husband a meaningful look as they stepped out of the closet and back to the party, where they ate and drank and exchanged an evening of pleasantries: veiled boasts and traded recipes, with the obligatory compliment thrown in here and there, before heading home in their car.

In their bedroom, she stood, staring at the sitting room. He joined her and tentatively put his arm around her waist.

"The closet *was* nice," he conceded. "And realistically, how often are we going to use this space?"

She was riding on BART with her co-worker. The car was hot and crowded.

"How's the reno coming?" her co-worker asked.

"Oh, fine," she said vaguely. "The contractor thinks they'll be finished next week."

"Aren't you glad you decided to put the closet in?" her co-worker asked.

"Oh, one hundred percent," she replied airily. "I don't know how he expected me to live without a walk-in."

One of the fellow riders, a woman dressed in a uniform, rolled her eyes and snorted. She realized that she and her co-worker probably sounded spoiled and shallow, but she didn't care. She smiled and looked out the window.

Days later, she stood in front of the finished closet. The empty shelves were laid out in front of her, like roads not chosen, full of potential and unexplored possibilities. She packed up her life into neat little compartments and began lining the shelves. Soon, everything was neatly arranged. Everything had a place. There was sense and meaning to it all. Finally, she put her wedding dress into a box and stuffed it in the back of the closet.

She smiled and shut the door.